"I know you're scared of someone. Who's following you, Faith?"

JT had no idea the dark secrets her mind had locked away because they were just too dreadful for her to remember. "I can't. I'm sorry, you don't understand."

A single muscle worked along his jaw line. Evidence enough he didn't like her answer. "Then help me understand. I take it this isn't the first time this has happened?"

She took her time answering. "No, it isn't. But it's my problem and I know what I'm doing."

"Like you have before? By being scared of everyone you meet? Always one step away from running? That's no way to live your life."

Faith squared her shoulders. "Maybe not, but I'll be okay. I appreciate your help tonight and for bringing my dog home, but this isn't your problem. I can handle it."

That he didn't believe her was clear. She couldn't blame him.

She desperately needed his help.

MARY ALFORD

grew up in a small Texas town famous for, well, not much of anything, really. Being the baby of the family and quite a bit younger than her brothers and sister, Mary had plenty of time to entertain herself. Making up stories seemed to come naturally to her.

As a preteen, Mary discovered writing and knew instinctively that was what she wanted to do with her overactive imagination.

She wrote her first novel as a teen (it's tucked away somewhere never to see the light of day), but never really pursued her writing career seriously until a few years later, when she wrote her first inspirational romantic suspense and was hooked.

Today, Mary still lives in Texas with her husband and still writes about romance. In fact, she can't think of anything else she'd rather do.

You can visit Mary at her website, www.maryalford.net, or email her at maryjalford@netzero.com.

FORGOTTEN PAST

MARY ALFORD

HARLEQUIN® LOVE INSPIRED® SUSPENSE

Recycling programs
for this product may
not exist in your area.

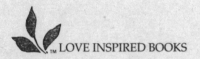

™ LOVE INSPIRED BOOKS

ISBN-13: 978-0-373-44604-9

FORGOTTEN PAST

www.Harlequin.com

Printed in U.S.A.

He gives power to those who are tired and worn out;
He offers strength to the weak.
—*Isaiah* 40:29

To my father-in-law, MJ Alford, who went home to be with the Lord December 6, 2012. God's gain, our loss. MJ, you taught me what it means to be a true hero because you were one to the people who loved you. I miss you terribly but I know that one day I'll see you again in Heaven, thanks be to God.

ONE

She'd made a dreadful mistake. The minute the headlights of her car swept over the house, Faith realized it deep down in her heart.

Truth be told, she had made a whole string of mistakes, including the one she prayed wouldn't prove to be the most costly. When she'd left the house earlier, she had forgotten to turn any lights on. Now night had fallen and nothing but a dark silhouette loomed before her. Just the thought of what might be waiting outside the safety of the car made her heartbeat go ballistic.

Please, Lord...protect me.

Faith clutched the steering wheel tight in an attempt to steady her trembling hands as she peered out the windshield. Nothing seemed out of place, but then again, it was pitch-black out. There were no streetlights this far from town, and dense clouds obscured the moon and stars. While the car's headlights illuminated most of the side of the house and a portion of the front, it didn't quite reach the door.

Foolish, foolish, foolish. She couldn't believe she'd acted so foolishly.

At the time, she hadn't thought about anything but getting away for a little while. The walls had been closing in on her, and she knew if she didn't find a way to clear her head, she would end up throwing everything she owned into the back of her car and running for her life once again.

Driving along the breathtaking stretch of Maine coastline while the setting sun painted the waters a kaleidoscope of colors helped put things into perspective. There was something about the never-ending cycle of the tide as it rolled against the rocky shoreline and then out to sea again that gave her a sense of peace. It reminded her that it didn't matter what she went through in her life, or how scary or insurmountable her fears seemed, God was in control.

Most days, she could control the doubts. Today hadn't been one of them. All because of the call. The reason she'd moved to Hope Island, a small town of a little more than ten thousand in population located at the southernmost tip of the Maine coastline. She had been running from *him*.

This move was supposed to be different. Faith had banked all her future happiness on it working this time. The call had proved her wrong. She had lost track of the number of times she'd uprooted her life just to get away from him. It had become second nature whenever she felt threatened. Today, when the call came in and the tiniest bit of hope she still clung to evaporated, she had definitely felt threatened.

At twenty-eight, Faith had given up two years of her life to this thing. She'd changed her name, her looks, shut herself off from the world as much as humanly possible, and yet each time he found her again.

She glanced up at the house and shivered at the possible dangers lying in wait inside.

Funny how something could appear so different when you were seeing it through the eyes of fear. Just a little more than a month earlier, she'd fallen in love with the old, two-story Cape Cod and rented it on the spot. Now, she could imagine him hiding in the enormous country kitchen, or lurking in the shadowy hallway.

Faith cracked the car's window and listened. Above the surging ocean waves beyond the house, nothing sounded unusual.

Yet something *wasn't* right. By now, Ollie would have recognized the sound of her vehicle and started barking like crazy.

She blew out a sigh. She couldn't stay out here all night. Maybe the call had truly been a wrong number this time.

Faith killed the engine, got out and hurried up the steps. She barely had time to put the key into the door when she heard it. Footsteps coming quickly up the stairs behind her. A shaft of light from a flashlight bounced off the porch and up the side of the house. Utterly unnerved, the hand holding her keys jarred away from her and the keys flew from her fingers.

"No." The word slipped from her tremulous lips.

She turned toward the light and the beam temporarily blinded her.

Faith had rehearsed this moment dozens of times in her head and yet the reality of it didn't feel anything like what she'd practiced.

Without the keys, the car would be useless, which left only one option. She'd need to make it to the back of the house. There were a handful of houses scattered along the stretch of beach behind her place. If she could reach one of them, hopefully someone would help her.

Faith raced toward the steps located off the side of the porch and away from the figure with the light.

There were three—no, four—steps leading down to the grassy yard. The fence separating her small backyard from the beach would be some fifteen feet behind the house. She'd carefully counted off each step her first day here.

"Wait."

She vaguely detected a deep male voice calling out to her when her right foot cleared the final step. She didn't dare look back. Her breath came in labored gasps as she rushed in the direction that she gauged the gate to be. Just a few more feet. Almost there.

His heavy footsteps echoed along the porch behind her. He was following her.

"Stop. I have your dog."

At first, her mind didn't register what he said. Every single thought focused on escaping. She bolted toward the beach, but she could hear her pursuer steadily gaining on her.

Faith reached for the latch on the gate when a strong hand clamped down on her shoulder. The momentum of his body slamming into hers sent them both sprawling along the dew-covered grass. It took a few seconds to drag air into her lungs and then she was kicking and punching him, fighting with everything she had, but her strength was no match for his.

"No!" she screamed as loud as she could, hoping someone would hear and come to her aid.

The stranger moved to a kneeling position, caught her flailing hands together in one of his, and brought them up over her head. "Stop that. I'm not going to hurt you." When she finally stopped struggling, he let her go and got to his feet.

"See? I mean you no harm," he said. Faith opened her eyes and stared at him for the first time. From her position lying flat on her back, he seemed incredibly tall.

She ignored the hand he held out to her. "Who are you? What do you want?"

"I told you, I have your dog."

"What are you talking about? My dog is inside my

house. How can you have him?" She sat up slowly, rubbing her wrists where he'd held them. In the darkness, she couldn't tell much from his expression.

"Well, his name tag says he's Ollie and that he lives here."

He knew her dog's name. While her brain struggled to make sense of it, barking coming from the front porch seemed to confirm his story. Yet Ollie was scared of his shadow. He would never willingly go to a stranger.

"Ollie, it's okay, boy. Come here." The little Pug bounded around the corner of the house and into her arms.

"Satisfied?" The stranger sounded amused. Faith got to her feet and put some distance between them, an impossible habit to break no matter how hard she tried. Another gift from *him*.

Although she couldn't remember a single thing about the actual attack that had taken place in Austin, she knew it had been brutal. When the EMTs brought her to the hospital, the doctor who treated her told her it had been so violent her mind had simply wiped away all traces of the incident as a coping mechanism. In spite of all her doctor's reassurances, her memory of the attack and what her life had been like before it remained locked away in her head.

She knew her attacker had murdered two people that night. Her friend Rachel Jennings and Rachel's father, Carl, had paid the ultimate price with their lives. Faith had given up a lot to this nightmare as well. She had nothing left to give except for her life and *he* seemed determined to take that from her as well.

She brushed off her jeans while Ollie wriggled in her arms and licked her nose. She could only imagine what this man must be thinking after their hot-pursuit chase. "Yes. I'm sorry. I thought…" She stopped, realizing she couldn't possibly tell him the truth. Most normal people would probably think *she* was the crazy one, and at this point, she was beginning to wonder if she was. She shook her head. "Never mind. Where did you find him?"

"Sitting on my back deck barking at the door and demanding to be let in. I guess he mistook my house for yours. He doesn't appear to see too well at night. I stopped by earlier, but no one was home. I took the dog for a walk on the beach and saw your car lights."

She smiled at his description of Ollie. At almost fourteen years old, a lot of things didn't quite work the way they used to. Ollie's poor eyesight was one of his latest ailments.

"Well, thank you for bringing him back. I don't know how he got out." Faith headed back toward her house with Ollie's rescuer falling into step beside her, careful to keep some space between them. He'd caught the way she reacted when he got too close.

"I'll help you find your keys. My name is JT Wyatt, by the way." He held out his hand and she hesitated only a second before accepting it.

"Faith McKenzie."

JT stepped up onto the porch and retrieved his flashlight from where he'd dropped it.

It took only a second to locate the keys beneath the porch swing. "Can you hold this for a second?" He handed her the light and got down on his knees to recover the keys. She caught a glimpse of faded jeans and a dark, long-sleeved turtleneck. The casual way he dressed didn't quite fit with her first impression of him. She hadn't pegged him as a local. More the corporate vacation type.

The light illuminated golden highlights scattered throughout his chestnut hair, which he wore swept back away from his face. A single strand fell across his forehead, dispelling the notion that he might have walked off the cover of some slick magazine.

"Here you go," JT said as he got to his feet. She realized her first assessment of him had been correct. He was tall—well over six feet. She had to tip her head back just to look him in the eyes. They were a magnificent shade of blue that reminded her of the sky on a summer day.

Faith tamped down her wayward thoughts. "Thank you."

He grinned at her. "No problem. I'm just glad I was home when Ollie showed up. I'd hate to think of him roaming around the beach on his own. October nights here can get pretty cold."

When JT handed her the keys, his fingers brushed against hers, sending an unwelcome jolt of awareness surging through her, and she instinctively took a step back. His gaze narrowed just a fraction as he watched her, no doubt witnessing all her anxiety. Faith turned away and unlocked the door while praying he wouldn't ask the questions she'd seen in his eyes.

"Looks like you have a secret admirer."

Immediately her heart leaped to her throat and she turned back to him. "Excuse me?"

JT pointed the flashlight at something just beyond the door. "Someone left you flowers."

A dozen red roses had been deliberately placed on the porch railing.

Faith struggled not to fall apart. In spite of what she'd hoped, she realized the call earlier *hadn't* been an accident. He wanted her to find the roses when she returned, but she had been too scared and intent on escaping her would-be attacker to see them right away.

This was *his* subtle little reminder he could find her

wherever she went. He enjoyed toying with her. The way a cat toyed with a mouse before devouring it.

"I take it you weren't expecting those." JT continued to watch her expression carefully.

"No."

He took the flashlight and went over to examine the flowers. Nothing unusual about the dozen red roses in a cut-glass vase except for their purpose. They were part of his deadly game.

"They were purchased at the local florist here on the island. There's a card attached." JT held it out to her.

She closed her eyes and tried to capture the faintest memory. There had once been a time when she'd loved red roses. Something had changed. The memory disappeared before she could grasp it. Had it been real?

When she opened her eyes, she realized JT still held the note. She couldn't bring herself to take it from him. Read the words aloud. Relive the terror again. When she shook her head, he placed the note back in its holder. "You should probably get them inside anyway. They'll be ruined by morning."

She shook off her uneasiness with difficulty. "Yes, you're right. Thank you." Faith took the roses from him even though she couldn't bear the sight of them. She'd throw them in the trash as soon as JT left.

"If you'd like, I could come inside and take a look around. Just to ease your mind."

Her hand stilled on the door. She hesitated. She didn't know what to trust anymore, including her own judgment. She should refuse JT's offer outright. Thank him for his kindness and send him on his way.

"That's very kind of you, but I don't think so."

When he stepped closer, her back hit the door and he stopped. "You're obviously frightened. I can check things out to make sure nothing's out of place and then I'll be on my way. If you want, you can wait out here until I'm finished. I promise I don't have any ulterior motives," JT added with a hint of a smile.

She knew she was being ridiculous. He only wanted to help. After all, he'd taken the time to bring Ollie home when the dog had wandered onto his back deck. JT seemed genuinely concerned about her well-being, and at some point in her life she needed to learn to trust someone if she wanted to live long enough to discover her attacker's identity.

Through every single one of the moves, she'd prayed for God's help. At times, it seemed as if He wasn't in the answering mood when it came to her prayers. At one of the church services she'd attended once, she remembered the pastor saying that God didn't always choose to answer prayers in the way we would like Him to, but He always answered them in the best way for us. Had God sent a total stranger into her life as an answer to her prayer?

Trust Me. The words echoed through her thoughts. Trust was a hard thing for Faith to give freely, but she needed to try.

"Okay," she said at last. "Thank you. I'd really like that." She stepped aside and let JT pass through.

Faith flipped on the lights. She set the roses on the table by the door and waited with Ollie while JT searched through each room of her house.

"Here's your problem," he called out from the kitchen. When she followed him to the room, he pointed to Ollie's pet door. "You forgot to lock it in place. The little guy probably figured out how to open it."

An unbelievable sense of relief soaked into every fiber of her body. "Oh, I'm so relieved. For a second, I thought…"

"That you had an intruder?" JT finished for her.

He obviously thought she'd overreacted. He had no way of knowing what she'd been through in her life to warrant such a response.

"Yes," she admitted and felt foolish. "I've only been here on the island a month. I guess I'm still getting used to living out here. Especially so far away from town."

"I see. Well, you don't have anything to worry about living here alone. This is one of the safest places to live in Maine. We rarely have anything more than the occasional high school prank."

So he *was* a local. This surprised her. "You live here?"

JT nodded. "Yes. I'm restoring the house down the beach from you." He was a carpenter. That explained the healthy tan. Still, it didn't quite fit her first impression of him.

JT had a funny little grin on his face and she realized she'd been staring again. "Well, thank you for rescuing Ollie," she said to cover up her embarrassment.

"No problem. I kind of admire the little guy's spunk." He reached down and scratched Ollie's ears, and the dog rewarded him with a lick on his hand.

Faith laughed warmly. "I think you've made a new friend. Ollie loves having his ears scratched."

When JT straightened, he looked right into her eyes and her heart did a little flip. He was an incredibly attractive man, yet she wondered if he even realized it.

He glanced away and she could breathe normally once more.

"You know, I remember this house. I came here a lot as a kid. My mom and the previous owners were friends. As I recall, Mom brought my sister and me over a couple of times a week for a visit. Liz and I used to explore the house while my mom and Evie Fitzgerald talked." He sighed fondly. "I remember Mrs. Fitzgerald used to make this mean chocolate cake and she'd give my sister and me each a huge slice. We would end up with a sugar rush for hours after. It drove our mom crazy."

She smiled as she listened to him reminisce about his family. She couldn't remember the last time she'd had such a simple conversation with anyone without looking for ulterior motives. It felt nice. "I can imagine. Are you and your sister still close?" Ollie scratched at her leg, his little signal he wanted her to hold him. She scooped the dog up in her arms.

"Oh, yes." He sounded amused. "Sometimes a little too close. Liz is happily married and determined that everyone around her should be as well. She's constantly trying to set me up on blind dates," he added with a shake of his head.

Faith found herself unexpectedly drawn to him. She liked the way his eyes lit up when he talked about his sister. It must be an incredible blessing to have someone to care about you in such a way. She'd been on her own for a long time and she'd never really known the love of a family. Since moving to Hope Island, her interactions with others had been limited to the cashier at the local grocery store and the occasional hello from the postal employee who sorted the mail.

"Actually, that sounds pretty nice." She stole a sideways glance at him and found him watching her with a sympathetic look on his face. When had she gotten so bad at covering up her feelings?

"Yes, I guess it is. As much as I tease my sister about being a mother hen, it's nice having her close. She and her husband, Sam, and my niece Ellie live here on the island as well, so I get to see them a lot." He hesitated. "I take it you don't have any family close by?"

Faith struggled against feelings of loneliness. She hated

being completely alone with no one to talk to about her problems and terrified of something she couldn't remember.

Before she could come up with an answer, JT held up his hands. "I'm sorry. I shouldn't have asked and it's none of my business. Here I am talking about Liz being nosy." He chuckled. "Blame it on the detective in me. I guess we're always searching for answers."

Faith did her best not to react to the news that he was a cop. After what happened in Austin and the way the detectives had treated her, she had stopped trusting in the police for help.

"You know, we can keep doing this all night," he said softly, interrupting her troubled thoughts.

She swallowed hard. "Doing what?" But she knew.

His expression gave nothing away. "Making polite conversation while we ignore what we should be talking about. Like who you really thought was following you tonight."

Faith couldn't hold his gaze.

"I know you're scared of someone. Who's following you, Faith?"

He had no idea the dark secrets her mind had locked away because they were just too ghastly for her to remember. "I can't. I'm sorry, you don't understand."

A single muscle worked along his jawline. Evidence enough he didn't like her answer. "Then help me understand. I take it this isn't the first time this has happened?"

She took her time answering. "No, it isn't. But it's my problem and I know what I'm doing."

That look on his face said that he didn't believe her, and she couldn't blame him. After all, the way she'd reacted tonight wasn't the normal behavior of someone who had things completely under control.

"I suppose you're right. It's not my place to—" Before

he could finish the sentence, her cell phone chirped to life on the kitchen counter where she'd left it earlier. Suddenly, she couldn't move. "Don't you think you should answer it?" JT asked when she made no attempt to do so. "It might be important." She read every single one of the questions in his eyes. She knew them all by heart.

After the third unanswered ring, JT picked up her cell phone and handed it to her, forcing her hand.

The caller ID registered "Unknown," just as it always did. Faith wanted to throw the phone as far away as she could, but if it were truly him, it wouldn't matter if she didn't answer. He would just keep calling...or worse.

It took everything inside her to accept JT's challenge without falling apart. "Yes. Yes, of course you're right." Her hands shook as she hit the talk button and listened to the familiar stanza of the old love song, "I'll Be Seeing You."

She murmured something to JT—some excuse—she wasn't sure what. Somehow, Faith managed to draw air into her lungs. Put one foot in front of the other. She needed distance between herself and the man watching her every move, seeing too much. If she wanted to stay alive, she couldn't fall apart. If she stayed in the same room with JT, she would.

Faith closed the door to the great room and leaned against it. "Please, please, just leave me alone," she whispered frantically. "I don't remember anything. I can't hurt you." The sound of a receiver slammed into its cradle was her only answer. She pushed away from the door and sank down to the sofa. Tears sprang easily to her eyes and she rubbed her hand over them.

She was so tired of fighting this battle alone.

"Is something wrong?" JT asked quietly from the doorway. She hadn't even heard him come in.

Faith rose to her feet and moved away before he could spot the tears. "No, I'm fine. It's…nothing."

"Then why are you crying?"

"I'm not—" She couldn't go on when he came over to where she stood and stopped inches away. JT touched his finger gently to her cheek and held up the proof for her to see.

"Who was that on the phone just now? What's really going on here, Faith?" The gentleness in his tone made it next to impossible to remain strong. It would be so nice to be able to lean on someone besides herself for a change. *Remember Austin. Remember how the police treated you there.*

She shook her head. "It was just a wrong number."

"That's not the truth, is it? Tell me what's going on in your life. I promise you can trust me."

She'd give anything to believe him, but she couldn't. Two people were dead already because of her, and she was no closer to learning the name of the person responsible for their murders now than on the night of the attack. Even if she did trust JT, she'd be putting his life in jeopardy by doing so. "I'm sorry, I can't."

JT glanced around the great room at the unpacked moving boxes scattered around the room. "You said you've been here a month and yet you're prepared to pick up and leave at a moment's notice. What are you running from, Faith McKenzie?" he said, a challenge in his voice.

She drew in a shaky breath and did her best to answer without giving anything else away. "Nothing."

Just the tiniest of smiles lifted the corners of his mouth. "I spent way too many years as a detective not to know when someone isn't telling me the truth. Whatever this is, it won't go away on its own."

When she didn't answer, he added, "Okay, I understand.

You're not ready, but when you are, you can talk to me." He glanced at his watch. "It's late and I should go, but if you need anything, anything at all, you can call me. I live just down the beach from you." He reached inside his wallet and pulled out a business card. "Here are my numbers. The one at the bottom is for the house here but you can reach me on my cell at any time, day or night."

"Wyatt Securities" jumped out at her in bold black lettering.

"I mean it, Faith. If you need anything, you call. Even if it's just to talk."

He walked over to the door before adding, "I'm going to give you a piece of free advice. Living on the island, especially out here along the beach, can be isolated. We are all neighbors here. We take care of and rely on each other. I don't know what's going on in your life, but if he's bad enough to make you as scared as you clearly are, I hope he doesn't follow you here to Hope Island for everyone's sake." JT lifted a finger in a final farewell then strode out her door and she could breathe again.

He had no way of knowing how much she desperately hoped for the same thing.

JT had seen the expression in Faith McKenzie's eyes a hundred times before while working domestic violence cases. It never got easier and it always promised a bad ending. Faith McKenzie was scared to death. God only knew what kind of trouble lurked in her past.

He'd encountered a lot of desperate victims on the job, but the type of fear he'd seen in her tonight seemed fused to every part of her being. He couldn't imagine what had happened in her life to bring her to this point.

JT tried to dismiss the unfamiliar stirring in his heart as he walked along the beach to his house. There was something about Faith that made him want to help her. No one deserved to live in such turmoil, and although she was clearly scared out of her mind, he couldn't deny he found himself attracted to her. He hadn't thought of another woman as beautiful since Emily's death.

Even without a trace of makeup, Faith was a strikingly lovely woman. She'd twisted her raven hair up into a makeshift knot on top of her head. Several strands had worked loose and framed her oval face. She hadn't been trying to impress anyone and yet she possessed the type of beauty that didn't need enhancing. But it was her eyes that tore at his heart the most. They were the color of midnight blue and haunted by fear.

Without a doubt, she was one troubled soul and he didn't know what to do about it.

You can't help someone who doesn't want your help, he could almost hear his sister saying. It was certainly true enough and it wasn't as if he didn't have his own set of concerns to worry about.

This had been the most stressful week in a long time and the upcoming one promised even more issues. One of Wyatt Securities' potential clients, a global energy firm, had recently detected a major security breach in their servers and had come to Wyatt for advice on how to overhaul their systems and to ferret out any additional breaches. If Wyatt landed the contract, it would mean a huge amount of business for the company. With their already heavy workload, the additional business added up to a lot of overtime for the staff and for JT. While part of him welcomed the challenge, lately he was feeling a little overwhelmed and unfulfilled. There had to be more to life than work. Even for someone like him.

JT rubbed a hand across his jaw. He had enough on his

plate figuring out his own life, so the *last* thing he needed right now was the kind of trouble Faith represented.

Lord, You help her. I can't. His prayer sounded about as empty as he felt inside. Truth be told, he had stopped looking to God for help after his wife's death. He wasn't even sure he believed anymore. After all, if God was so all-powerful and loving, why had He let someone good like Emily die in such a brutal way? JT himself should have been the one to walk into that convenience store and confront the robber. He should have died that night. Not her. Yet for his sister's sake, he still attended the small church they'd grown up in each week and pretended. But the pastor's message, the scriptures he read—they didn't reach into his heart the way they had in the past.

The house JT had been restoring here on the island for the past three years had become his only real source of contentment.

His father had been a local Hope Island police officer for more than twenty years and had taught JT how to find comfort in the simple things of life. After Edward Wyatt retired from the force, he'd begun restoring houses up and down the Maine coast. JT loved working with his father. He'd never felt closer to him than when they were working side by side to bring something on the brink of ruin back to its former glory.

JT reached the edge of his property and turned toward the house he'd just left.

Who exactly had been on the other end of that call to bring such terror to Faith McKenzie's eyes? The way she reacted to his sudden appearance, even after she realized he posed no threat, pointed to someone who didn't know her stalker's identity. If so, then every stranger she met would represent a possible risk.

The detective in him wanted to know what she was hiding in her past. A woman so young didn't move to an isolated town like Hope Island without just cause.

Whatever it was, it has nothing to do with you, he said to himself. He had offered his help. If she didn't accept it, there wasn't much else he could do.

Still, out of curiosity, JT grabbed his cell phone and called Derek Thomas, his good friend and one of the founding members of Wyatt Securities.

"Hey, I need you to do me a favor," JT said without bothering to return Derek's hello. "Can you do a background check on someone?"

It wasn't unusual for JT to ask for Derek's help in this manner. After all, he was a computer genius and could uncover anyone's secrets no matter how deeply hidden. "Sure, pal, whatever you need. Who do you want me to check on?"

"Her name is Faith McKenzie. She rented the old Fitzgerald house down the beach from me."

"I see. What's your concern with her?" He could tell from Derek's tone that he thought it odd JT wanted a background check done on his neighbor.

"I'm not sure." He briefly filled in his friend on the chase that ensued after he stopped by Faith's place to return her dog to her. "From her over-the-top reaction, I think someone is stalking her and my gut tells me this isn't the first time it's happened, either."

Six months after his wife's death, JT had left the police force because he couldn't bear the constant reminder of how he'd let Emily down. He'd founded Wyatt Securities along with Derek and another close friend, Teddy Warren. He hadn't been able to help Emily, but he was determined not to let such a tragedy befall another innocent person on this island.

"I want to know what she's hiding. If it's any help, she

has a very distinctive Texas accent. She's obviously lived there at some time in her past."

After a slight hesitation, Derek said, "I'll get started on it right away."

"Good. What were you up to before I interrupted your evening?" JT could hear the TV in the background.

"Listening to the Weather Channel mostly. There's a tropical storm building strength in the Atlantic."

JT blew out a sigh. "Yeah, I heard." The storm in question was all over the radio lately. Every time the Weather Bureau issued a warning, people up and down the coast went on full alert. With everything going on at work, this was the last thing JT needed. If the storm kept gaining strength, he'd have to stockpile necessities and weather-proof the house just in case.

"If it keeps on the path it's on now, the entire East Coast is within its strike zone. Who knows where it'll hit. I'm still praying it will lose strength before it gets close." Derek paused. "Well, I'd better get a move on. I'll give you a call as soon as I have something on your neighbor."

"Thanks, buddy. I don't know what I'd do without you." JT disconnected the call and unlocked the back door. As he stepped inside the house, his cell phone rang again. Liz's number popped up on the caller ID. She worried about him; that's what big sisters did. He touched the ignore button. He would call her back tomorrow. Right now, he couldn't get his mind off the terrified woman down the beach.

Was he simply trying to find redemption for failing Emily by helping a stranger in need? Possibly, yet there was something different about Faith McKenzie.

Get her out of your mind, Wyatt. You have plenty of real concerns in your life to be worried about. He grabbed his laptop and cleared off enough space at the kitchen table to set up shop, while ignoring the reminders scattered around the house of things he should be doing. Like finishing the drywall in the great room, not to mention getting the cabinets hung in the kitchen so he could finally put dishes away.

Instead, he started brewing a pot of coffee and dove into work. In the security world, business was booming. On average, over the past year, the company had a couple of new clients sign on every month. If things kept growing at this rate, he would need to hire additional staff just to keep up.

JT was halfway through writing a proposal for the global energy firm when Derek called back.

"That was fast."

As usual, his friend didn't mince words. "It took some doing, but I was able to find a copy of her lease agreement for the house. Since the Fitzgeralds didn't have any living relatives, the county commissioned a real estate agency to sell the house. In the current market, selling a house that size is next to impossible so the agency agreed to put it up for rent, which meant the agreement was on file at county records." Derek cleared his throat. "Apparently, the leasing agent didn't do a credit check, because the name McKenzie didn't match up with the social security number on the application. That social corresponds to a Faith Davenport who was originally from Oklahoma City, but moved to Austin, Texas when she was a teenager."

This bit of news wasn't a surprise. "Figures. She changed her name because she's running from someone."

"Probably," Derek confirmed. "Her past is sketchy. Parents died when she was ten and she ended up in foster care. She ran away to Texas when she was a teenager. It appears she turned her life around. Finished school and got an accounting degree from the University of Texas—all online.

She doesn't appear to have much of a presence online now. I'm still digging. I'll know more soon."

"Good."

"So what are you thinking about doing?" Derek asked the expected question. He knew JT well enough to know he hadn't wanted the information just to satisfy his curiosity.

JT stared out the kitchen window. In the darkness, all he could see was his own troubled reflection. "I'm not sure, but if anyone needs our help it's Faith McKenzie."

TWO

Somewhere close by, a ringing noise woke Faith from a sound sleep. She had forgotten to turn off her phone.

She sucked in a handful of frightened breaths as the phone continued to shrill. Three more rings followed by dead silence and then the real trepidation set in.

Ollie let out a low growl and moved closer to Faith's side.

"It's okay, boy." If only that were true, but dread settled on her shoulders like a prickly blanket because she had been here before. This was the third call. At this point in the past, she'd be tossing everything she owned into the back of her car and running before he had the chance to make his next move. Only this time he'd changed the game. He'd sent her roses already. So why was he stepping up the threats now, after two years?

An eternity passed before her eyes adjusted to the darkness. Over the staccato beat of her heart, she heard it. The sound of a car's engine. Someone was outside.

Panic pumped adrenaline through her body, propelling her out of bed. She clutched Ollie close and tiptoed over to the window. Her bedroom faced the ocean instead of the driveway. She could see headlights shining off the side of the house and out toward the water.

She didn't know what to do. She'd stopped trusting the cops long ago. The Austin police hadn't believed her when she'd first reported the calls to the detectives handling her case. They'd all but accused her of making the whole thing up to get attention. Or worse.

Faith crept downstairs with Ollie tucked under her arm. She didn't dare turn on any lights. She had practiced getting around the house without them many times.

When she reached the great room, she inched the drapes apart. A pickup truck sat motionless in her driveway. Lights turned on bright. The engine revved up. It sounded as if the person inside had the gas pedal all the way to the floor.

Faith groped her way over to where she'd left JT's business card. Using the light from her phone, she called the cell number listed there. After the third ring, he picked up. At the husky sound of his voice she let go of the breath she'd been holding.

"JT Wyatt." Too late, she wondered if she might have awakened him from a sound sleep.

"I'm sorry to call so late, but I didn't know what else to do. There's someone outside my house." Panic infused its way into every syllable she spoke.

"I'm on my way. Where are you?" He didn't hesitate to offer his help.

"I'm in the great room."

"Good. Stay there and don't open the door until you hear me call out to you."

The phone went silent. He hadn't waited for her answer, but it didn't matter. Just knowing he was on his way was a tremendous relief.

She double-checked the front door to make sure it was securely locked and then went back to the great room, expecting the showdown she had known was coming since that night two years ago.

JT shoved the phone back into his pocket and raced toward Faith's house. He'd been down the beach from her place when the call came in. After tossing and turning most of the night, he'd finally abandoned sleep altogether around four a.m. It was still dark outside when he'd decided to take a walk, mostly because there were too many questions running through his head. He'd begun working the details of her case from the minute he met her. Saw the terror in her eyes, the way she reacted to him. Added to that were the clues he'd seen lying around her house, and there'd been plenty. She'd gone for overkill with three locks on both doors. A state-of-the-art security system, stun gun, enough pepper spray to stop a small army.

All those things pointed to someone who had gotten good at being on the run. Faith McKenzie was in big trouble. The kind of trouble that didn't go away on its own, but convincing her to let him help her wasn't going to be easy. She was about as closed up emotionally as anyone he'd ever seen.

When he reached the edge of her property, he clicked off the flashlight he'd brought with him and stopped long enough to listen for any unusual noises. He could hear a truck engine coming from the front of her house. JT circled around to the drive. The truck's headlights bounced off the side of the house and JT ducked behind a nearby shrub. The driver didn't appear concerned about all the noise he was making, which told JT he'd done his homework. The closest house to Faith's was his and he was a quarter mile down the beach. Far enough away for the noise from the ocean to drown out the sound of the truck.

JT couldn't see the driver. It took him only a second to

realize why. The windows of the truck had been tinted dark and there didn't appear to be any dash lights on. Someone had deliberately disconnected them to prevent anyone from seeing inside the truck.

JT counted to three, drew the Glock he carried in his jacket pocket and then stepped out from behind his cover. The vehicle didn't move. The engine kept on revving.

"Get out of the truck. Now," he shouted but the driver ignored his command. Something was definitely off. JT skirted around the back of the truck to the driver's side and knocked on the window. Nothing. He tried the door and it opened without effort. There was no one inside. Someone had placed a brick on the accelerator pedal to ensure that the engine ran at full throttle.

JT reached inside and turned off the ignition and the truck coughed to a sputtering death. Why had someone left it idling in her driveway?

The hair on the back of JT's neck suddenly stood up with the realization that this had been a setup. Whoever did this was deliberately trying to lure Faith outside. They'd probably been watching her movements for a while.

The headlights would provide enough light for the person to see that JT wasn't Faith, which meant…JT slammed the door shut and charged for the cover of the shrubs as the first barrage of bullets split the silence.

He counted off five rapid rounds from what sounded like an AK-47. The bullets kicked up dirt and bits of gravel. He could feel them pepper his back and legs. He dove for the closest bush as another barrage of bullets flew past his body. A couple hit the side of the house and lodged in the siding.

JT crouched low to the ground and scrambled toward the back of the house while the shooter continued to fire. He made it to the back deck and inched up onto the porch out of the shooter's line of sight. Faith was in the great room located in the front of the house. He'd told her not to open the door until he called out. With the noise of the ocean and the steady repeat of gunfire, she'd never hear him.

He grabbed his phone and hit Redial.

She answered right away. "JT, what's going on? I heard gunshots. Are you okay?"

He drew much-needed air into his lungs before answering, "I'm okay for now but I'm at the back of the house. I need you to get to the door and unlock it as soon as you can. Hurry, Faith, I'm not sure if he followed me."

JT rushed to the back door. If his assailant came after him now, he wouldn't stand a chance.

"I'm almost there now," she said.

His heartbeat ticked off every second before he heard her fumbling with the locks and then the door opened. She turned on the light switch. Nothing happened. Someone had flipped off the breakers.

JT locked the door, shoved the Glock back into his pocket and grabbed Faith's arm. He headed for the one room without windows he remembered from his childhood, a small laundry room off the kitchen. Once they were both inside, he shut the door and pushed a couple of heavy boxes in front of it.

"What happened out there? Who was in the truck?" Faith's questions tumbled out, her eyes wide with fear.

JT didn't answer right away. He listened for a second and heard nothing but silence outside. The gunshots had stopped. "That's just it, there was no one in the truck. It sounded like the shots came from the outcropping of trees across the road. He cut the power to the house trying to draw you out." A muscle ticked in his jaw. "However, what he wasn't expecting was me. We need to call the police right away. We're sitting ducks and he could still be out there."

Before he could say anything more, she was busily shaking her head. "No. No police, I don't trust them."

JT watched her for a second. Even though she hadn't said as much, it was easy to read between the lines. She had gone to the cops for help in the beginning and they'd let her down.

He tried to soften his tone. "If he comes after us with that kind of firepower, I don't know if I can keep you alive. We have to call the police. Let me do this, Faith."

A handful of tension-filled seconds passed before she finally agreed.

He grabbed his phone and called the number of one of his closest friends and the chief of police for Hope Island.

"What's wrong?" Chief Will Kelly didn't bother with hello. JT wouldn't be calling at six in the morning unless it was urgent.

"I'm at the old Fitzgerald place with the new tenant. Someone is shooting at us with a high-powered weapon. He's taken out the power to the place, Will. I don't know if he's still there or if he's acting alone. We need help ASAP." A split second later, he heard Will bark out instructions to the police dispatcher. "Terry, shots fired at 21 Ocean Way. There are two people inside the old Fitzgerald house. We don't know if the gunman is still on the premises. We need whoever's on duty now over there right away. Let them know they may be walking into an ambush. Vests on and everyone watch their backs…"

He came back to JT after he finished putting the order in motion. "Help is en route. Dispatcher Terry Hendricks says that Samuels and Kennedy are five minutes out. Hang in there, I'm on my way as well. The first patrol cars should be there any minute. Just stay put until reinforcements get there."

No sooner had he disconnected the call than a siren blared in the distance.

Within a matter of minutes, the first patrol car descended on the house. JT had no doubt the person doing the shooting would be in the wind by now.

He moved the boxes away from the door and they crept out to the dark kitchen. Police lights strobed the side of the house. Seconds later, the whole outside was lit up as bright as daylight and the team began to scour the area for the shooter.

Someone knocked loudly on the door and JT turned on the flashlight and went to the front of the house with Faith following close behind, clutching the dog. He opened the door to find Will and two uniformed officers standing there. Will ducked his head as he entered the house. At almost six-nine, this action had obviously become second nature for him.

His friend combed back a stray lock of bright-red hair and shook JT's hand. "Sounds like you two have had a bit of excitement this morning."

"That's putting it mildly," JT said as he stepped aside and the three men came inside. "Will, this is Faith McKenzie. She's renting the house. Faith, this is Chief Will Kelly."

The chief of police held out his hand. "It's nice to meet you, Faith." After only the slightest hesitation, she took it. Will turned to the two uniformed officers. "Take a look around back. See if anything has been disturbed. Be careful."

"Thank you for coming so quickly, Chief Kelly," Faith said.

"It's Will, and you're welcome. We have officers searching for the shooter and forensics will be here shortly to examine the truck. In the meantime, I'll need to ask you both some questions, starting with what exactly took place here this morning."

The reality of what had happened struck Faith like a blow. This wasn't just a matter of overreacting. Jumping at shadows. The threat had been all too real, and it had almost had very deadly consequences.

Now, with both men staring at her, waiting for answers, she wasn't so sure she could go through with it. What if they didn't believe her or thought she was involved, as the Austin police had?

"I don't think I can do this," she whispered to JT.

He reached for her hand and held on to it. "Yes, you can. I promise you can. I'll be right here with you through it all. Will and I aren't going to let anything bad happen to you, Faith."

"You can't make that promise."

JT turned to Will. "Can you give us a moment?"

Chief Kelly glanced from one to the other before finally agreeing. "Sure. I'll just go check on the progress outside."

JT waited until they were alone. "You've been through a lot tonight. You need a second to gather your thoughts. Why don't we go to the great room and sit for a little while?"

She readily agreed because she desperately needed to soothe her frayed nerves.

JT turned on his flashlight once more and she followed him inside and closed the door. The room appeared eerie as the flashlight's beam leaped along the walls.

They sat together on the sofa without saying a word. When JT turned off the light the room was plunged into darkness, but that was okay because he was there with her, holding her hand. For the first time in a long time, she felt safe.

For just a little while, she wanted to be still. Calm the storm roiling inside. She wanted the world around her to stop spinning out of control. Wanted the nightmare to end.

JT touched her arm. "You're shivering." He turned in his seat to see her better. "It *is* cold in here."

He started to untangle his hand from hers but she held on tighter. "No, please don't go. I really don't want to be alone."

"I'm not going anywhere. I'm just going to make a fire to take the chill away." She let go of his hand and he clicked the flashlight and got to his feet. JT crumpled some old newspaper in the fireplace for kindling and then stacked wood on top. Within seconds after lighting the kindling, the fire was burning in the grate and the room became bathed in its warm glow.

He sat down next to her once more. "I need you to listen to me." The gentleness in his tone forced her to do as he asked. "I know you're scared, but we have to know what's going on here if we're going to help you. This—whatever it is—has gone way beyond what you can control on your own any longer. I need you to trust me, Faith."

A tiny sob escaped from deep inside her. "I do trust you."

"Then let me help you. Tell me what's happening."

"I can't. I'm sorry, but I can't. JT, you almost died this morning because I asked for your help. I couldn't bear it if anything happened to you. I can't let anyone else die for me."

The compassion in his intense blue eyes amazed her. "Did someone you love die because of the person who was shooting outside?"

"Yes," she whispered at last.

"I know this is hard…trust me, I understand what it's like to lose someone close to you in a violent way. I was married once. My wife was murdered."

She'd wondered about his past. He had an aura of sadness surrounding him. She'd noticed it when he brought Ollie back the night before. Yet nothing prepared her for hearing his wife had been killed. "Oh, JT, I'm so sorry. That must have been…horrible."

He lowered his head. She couldn't see his eyes but his voice flattened when he answered. "It was the hardest thing I've ever had to live through and it's not something I like to discuss. In fact, you're the first person I've shared this with beyond my family and closest friends. For the longest time after Emily's death, I wasn't so sure I was going to make it through. I hated the world and blamed everyone, including myself, for her death." His words grew thick with emotion. "But I *did* make it through…with the help of my family and friends."

When he looked at her, she didn't make a sound, but gazed deep into his eyes, encouraging him to continue.

"You see, I realized I couldn't do it on my own. I needed help. It is possible to get your life back, Faith. Maybe even to be happy again, but you can't do it alone. It's one of the most valuable lessons I learned. At some time or other, we all need help. Let me help. Let Will."

Ollie let out a pitiful whimper and she realized she was squeezing him tight. She released the dog and he went over to investigate something close by.

She knew what JT said was true, but still, giving up the one thing that had kept her alive these past two years wasn't going to be easy.

She silently recited one of her favorite verses from the Bible.

Let not your heart be troubled. You believe in God, believe also in Me...

Those simple words gave her a sense of calm. Nothing was too great or powerful for God. Not even this.

The one blessing to come from this nightmare was that she had started attending a small church in the Midwest on one of her previous moves and had found God. She was slowly learning how to accept His guidance for her life, but at times, it wasn't easy to let go. Trust. None of those things came easy to her.

Off in the distance, thunder rumbled low and ominous above the crashing waves. A storm was approaching. The ocean had a way of drawing them to it. In the morning, everything would be clean and fresh and filled with promise.

If only her life could be like that.

She rose, went to the window and opened the drapes. It was just getting light outside. There were several officers combing the yard and the surrounding area. They'd left the truck parked in the middle of her drive—yet another reminder of the danger stalking her. A forensics team was examining every inch of the abandoned vehicle, dusting for prints.

She let the drapes fall back in place. "Do you believe God has a plan for our life?"

Her question clearly surprised him. He came over to where she stood. "Yes, I guess I do, although I confess, sometimes I have a hard time understanding His plan."

She felt the same way at times, but she truly believed God had a purpose for her as well. There had to be a reason why He'd led her here to Hope Island.

"It will be okay, Faith. I know it doesn't seem so right now but it will." He hesitated a second, then gathered her close and she let him because it seemed as natural as taking her next breath. In just a short amount of time, he'd become her safe haven and she held on to him.

"Are you ready to talk to my friend?"

She looked up at JT and saw the strength she needed. "Yes."

"Good. I'll go get him." He'd taken only a couple of steps toward the door when the overhead light flickered once and came on. The power was restored almost as if it were a sign.

JT turned back to her. Their gazes met and she held her breath. The warmth in his eyes held so many possibilities.

"It may take some time, but we'll find out who's doing this to you and we'll give you back your life again."

With his help, she believed they would.

THREE

Chief Will Kelly did his best to put her at ease, but the two police officers standing guard outside the great room only served to emphasize the dangerous nature of her situation.

JT took the seat next to her. Even though he hadn't said a word, having him close made her feel like she wasn't alone anymore.

"Why don't you start with what happened this morning? When did you first become aware something was wrong?" Chief Kelly opened his notebook and fished out a pen from his pocket.

"When I got the call this morning. It woke me up."

JT's gaze collided with hers. With everything that had happened since then, she'd forgotten to tell him about the phone call.

"He called again?" Something in his expression sent a shiver down her spine. The news of the call clearly surprised him, which meant what? That he didn't think her stalker's behavior was true to form?

"Yes," she answered at last. "Right before I heard the truck outside."

Will looked from Faith to JT. "Back up a little bit. What calls are we talking about here?"

"He—whoever's been doing this—has been calling me

for over two years now. He never speaks. There's always a song playing in the background."

The chief was busily taking notes. "What song?"

"'I'll Be Seeing You.' It's always the same."

"And he's never spoken?" The disbelief on Will's face made it hard for her to go on.

She squared her shoulders and looked him in the eye. "That's right." She had seen that same expression on the Austin detectives' faces whenever she'd first told them about the calls.

Faith still couldn't believe everything that had happened since the call woke her and she'd reached out to JT for help.

Will stopped writing. "By the way, the breaker box around the side of the house was flipped off, which explains why the power was off. We're dusting for prints, but I'm not holding out much hope. We ran the truck's plates. It was stolen out of a junkyard in Portland two weeks earlier."

Two weeks. Fear coiled into the pit of her stomach like a venomous snake. She couldn't believe it. He'd been stalking her, planning this move all this time, and she'd had absolutely no idea he'd found her again until the call came in yesterday.

Will flipped his notebook closed. "I'm guessing he stashed another vehicle on the main road. That's how he was able to get away so quickly. My men are combing the area for any evidence, but he's obviously good at this. Who knows how long he's been watching you." He paused and she knew what was coming next. The moment of truth. She'd been expecting it. Dreading it. "But then, I have a feeling you've been here before. Haven't you, Faith?"

She could feel the color drain from her face. She said a quick prayer and a sense of peace came over her. It was as if God was right beside her, telling her it was okay to let go. She didn't have to do this on her own anymore. "Yes, I've been here before. Many times, in fact."

Will held her gaze. "Who's doing this to you?"

At times, she'd give anything to know the answer to the chief's question, and at others, well, she wasn't so sure she could survive the truth.

Every time she thought about the interview with the Austin police, she shuddered. They'd all but accused her of being part of the Jennings' murders. They'd detained her at the station for hours until she'd finally asked for an attorney and then they'd let her go. She'd been terrified they would arrest her for the crime. Terrified they might be right.

"That's just it. I don't know who's doing this."

"I think you'd better explain," Will said.

She nodded slowly. "Two years ago, when I lived in Austin, I was attacked and badly beaten. My throat was slit. I almost died and the worst part of it all is I don't remember a single thing about the incident."

Will appeared lost. She couldn't blame him. If she hadn't lived through the nightmare, she'd probably think she'd lost her mind.

"Believe me, I know how crazy this sounds, but it's true. I don't remember anything about what happened."

"You mean you've blocked out the memories of the attack," JT offered.

She shook her head. "I mean I can't *remember* anything about it or my past. Nothing. Not a single thing."

When her memory hadn't returned after a few weeks, her doctors were at a loss for answers. They'd told her most victims of violent crimes who suffered temporary amnesia usually regained their memories in a matter of weeks and the amnesia certainly never encompassed other parts of their lives.

"I'm so sorry. I can't imagine what that must be like." The gentleness in JT's tone brought a lump to her throat. "What did the police say? Did they have any suspects? An old boyfriend? An acquaintance? Someone you were having trouble with around that time?"

At first, the police had seemed genuinely baffled, but it didn't take long before they started hinting at the possibility she was lying about not remembering because she might be mixed up in the murders. For them, it had been the only plausible explanation. And by the time she left Austin for good, they didn't bother hiding the fact they believed she was responsible for her friends' murders. One of the detectives had told her that the only thing keeping her out of jail was the lack of evidence he was sure they'd come up with eventually.

She shook her head. "Since I wasn't able to remember the attack, there were no suspects."

Will frowned at her answer. "So there's never been anyone charged with the assault?"

"No." On top of being terrorized by her stalker, she'd lived in constant fear the police might be right. Maybe she'd blocked out the memories because she was the real monster. But if that were true, then why was someone stalking her?

"How soon after the attack did the calls first begin?" Will asked.

"Not long, maybe about a week after I was released from the hospital." She hated thinking about those awful days following the attack. Her fear consumed her. Every time she looked at her reflection in the mirror she saw the evidence of how close to death she'd come. She was so battered and bruised she could barely walk. She'd been so afraid she couldn't leave the apartment for days after. She didn't know if the person responsible for killing the

Jenningses might be waiting for her to leave the apartment so he could finish the job.

She realized Will was analyzing her every reaction. "Tell me exactly how the calls started."

It had all begun so innocently. "It started with just a few hang-ups. At first I thought maybe someone from my past didn't recognize my voice." Both men looked confused and she explained. "I'm an accountant so I had people call in from time to time to ask questions. One of my clients told me I didn't sound like myself when he called. The injury damaged my vocal cords. My voice was…off. Huskier, I guess. Anyway, I assumed the calls were harmless until the music started and somehow I just knew it had to be him."

"When you reported this to the police, what did they say?" JT asked.

It was hard for her to keep from showing her resentment. "They didn't believe me. They pretty much accused me of making the whole thing up. I was terrified. I begged them to do something. They said their hands were tied until they actually caught the person committing an act of violence against me."

"I don't understand why they wouldn't believe you. You almost died from a brutal attack. The person who hurt you was obviously still at large, so it would be a reasonable assumption to connect the calls to the attack." Will narrowed his eyes at her. "What aren't you telling us, Faith?"

She shook her head. She couldn't tell them everything— it was just too ugly. "The police never believed my amnesia was real. They thought I might be using it as an excuse to keep from telling them what I knew about the attack."

"In other words, they thought you knew more than what you were saying," the chief concluded.

"Yes."

"And do you?"

The room grew quiet. Tension slithered down her spine. For a little while, she'd actually believed this time might be different, but one look at the skepticism on Will's face shattered her hopes. He thought she was lying. Would JT feel the same? How could she ever convince them she wasn't guilty when even she had doubts.

Faith got to her feet and headed for the door. "This was a mistake. I shouldn't have gotten you involved in this. I'm sorry I wasted your time."

She made it to the hallway when JT caught up with her and reached for her arm, preventing her from leaving. "Don't do that."

She closed her eyes for a second then turned to face him. "Do what?" she asked wearily.

"Give up on us. Me. Please don't lose hope, Faith."

The sincerity in JT's eyes reached past the wall of self-preservation she wore around her like armor.

"He doesn't believe me, JT, and I can't blame him. Don't you think I know how crazy all this sounds?"

He tugged her closer, she went into his arms, and he held her close. As she burrowed her head against his shoulder, it scared her how right this all felt. It was as if nothing bad in the world could ever reach her when she was in his protective embrace.

"Will's just doing his job. If he didn't ask a few hard questions, I wouldn't want him working the case. I trust him, Faith. You can, too."

She believed him. "Okay," she said at last.

"Good." JT took her hand and they went back to the great room where the chief waited for them.

"I know this is hard. I'm just trying to understand the details of the case. I'm not judging you," Will offered with a faint smile. "So, let's start again. Did you know more about the case than what you told the police?" he repeated.

"No." That was certainly true enough. She had told the police everything she knew about what happened and they hadn't believed her.

"So when they offered no help you did what you had to do to survive. You ran. I take it you've been running ever since."

She glanced down at her clasped hands. "Yes. I didn't know what else to do. I changed my name from Davenport to McKenzie, yet every time I thought I was safe, he found me again." She was so exhausted. She wasn't sure she had it in her to run anymore.

"How many times have you been forced to move?"

She'd almost lost track of the times she'd packed up and taken off for parts unknown. "Counting Hope Island, there have been seven."

Will didn't try to hide his surprise as he chose his next words carefully. "So you're telling me that you uproot your entire life because of these crank calls? Seems a bit extreme. Something else must have happened. What's the real reason why you've relocated all those times?"

Instinctively, she reached for JT's hand and held on to it. He turned to her. The warmth in his eyes seeped into the cold places inside where her fear lived, melting away her doubts. She was safe with him. She hadn't felt safe in a long time.

JT squeezed her hand. "You're doing great. Take your time."

She took a deep breath before telling them the details of that horrific time. "It started right after the third call in Austin. He broke into my apartment and left a picture of my friend Rachel and me on my dining room table. In Billings, I came home from work and found a candlelit dinner waiting for me. In Newport, Oregon, he left a bloody knife on my doorstep. Then in Kansas, he snuck into my apartment and watched me sleep one night."

Faith shuddered at the memory, but the look of encouragement on JT's face compelled her to continue. "When I woke up and saw him there, I was terrified. He wore a mask and the room was dark so I couldn't see his face, but I knew it was him. He didn't say a word. As soon as I acknowledged his presence, he left. I think he just wanted me to know he could get to me anytime he wanted."

"Hold on," Will interrupted. "You said it was dark and he wore a mask, but do you remember if he was tall or short? Was he stocky or slim?"

Faith thought about it for a second. "I'd say medium height, not quite six foot, and he had a slim build."

"It's something. Go on."

She shook her head. "The roses from yesterday are just the beginning. The method varies, but it's all part of the same twisted game." Yet something *was* different this time. She'd turned to someone for help. Now she'd reached out to the police. And unlike all those other times, her stalker now seemed determined to finish what he'd started two years earlier.

"What roses?" Will asked.

She realized he had no idea what she was talking about. "He left a dozen roses on my porch last night."

Will digested this new piece of information. "Where are they now? I'll need to see them."

"They're in the trash can behind the house. I couldn't bear to look at them," she added in response to JT's surprised expression.

He nodded. "I wish I'd known. About the flowers. About everything. I wouldn't have left you alone."

Her breath caught in her throat at the compassion she saw in him. Just for a second, as they stared into each other's eyes, it felt as if it could have been just the two of them. Nerves, awareness and something she couldn't begin to name flitted into the pit of her stomach.

Close by, Will cleared his throat.

JT untangled his gaze from hers and looked at his friend. "The flowers were from Stedman's downtown. There was a card attached as well."

"What'd it say?" Will asked her.

Those chilling words had kept her awake long into the night. Her voice shook as she repeated them. *"You belong to me and I want what's mine. I'll be seeing you soon."* She shivered when she thought of how he'd been right outside her front door. It was as if he enjoyed finding new ways to torment her.

She could tell from Will's reaction this didn't sit well with him. "I'll see if I can find out something from the owner. Maybe she'll remember who ordered the roses. I take it they don't have any particular meaning for you?"

"I hate to sound like a broken record, but I don't know. I have no idea why he sent them. For an instant, when I first saw them, well, I thought I recognized something about them, but now I'm not so sure. Maybe I just want to remember something…anything."

Will hesitated then said, "Up until now, it appears he wanted to keep you frightened and running for your life. That's changed. He's figured out you're actually talking to someone, maybe even remembering something from the attack, which means he's scared."

"Go on," she said, listening as if her life depended on it.

"Well, he knows what's locked away in your memory is enough to put him behind bars for a long time. Now that you've turned to us for help, he's going to feel even more threatened. Whatever reason he had to let you live in the past is suddenly null and void. You're a liability now."

As the reality of what Will said finally sank in, Faith wondered if she had just made the worst mistake of her life by asking for help.

Dear God, she hoped not.

JT squeezed her hand again. "You did the right thing, Faith. Remember, you're not alone anymore. You have us. We're not going to let anything happen to you."

She desperately wanted to believe him, but she'd seen firsthand how dangerous her assailant could be...and how determined. For over two years, he'd patiently stalked her as an animal stalked its prey. He'd proven he wasn't going away until one of them was dead.

She was barely holding it together as it was. She couldn't stand it if anything happened to JT or Will because she'd reached out to them for help.

"I'll have a couple of my men stationed outside the house tonight. I promise you'll be safe," Will added when he saw her frightened expression. "I can't even fathom how traumatic this has been for you, Faith, but one thing is bothering me. How does he keep finding you? Have you kept in touch with anyone from your old life? A friend, someone from work maybe. Anyone who might have unknowingly given away your whereabouts to the stalker?"

Admitting she was all alone in the world was hard. When she first got home from the hospital, she had no idea what her life had been like before. What she liked, what she didn't, so she'd dug into her past prior to the attack. Faith discovered she'd lived a very solitary life, working from home as an accountant. She didn't know her neighbors and had very little contact with the outside world. With the exception of Ollie, Rachel Jennings might very well have been her only friend.

"No. There's no one."

Will glanced at JT. "I don't like it. There has to be some

way he's keeping track of Faith. Is this the same cell phone you've had since Austin?"

His question surprised her. She hadn't considered the possibility he might track her through her phone. "Yes it is, but I've changed my number each time I've moved. Do you think that's how he's able to keep finding me?"

"I don't know, but it would certainly make sense. I'm going to have one of my techs check the phone for any tracking devices." Will grabbed his cell phone and spoke briefly to someone. "Do I have your consent to have your calls traced?"

"Of course," she agreed. "Anything you need."

"Good. If we can keep him on the line long enough, we might be able to find out where he is."

A huge weight lifted from her shoulders and hope took root. She quickly quashed it. It was too soon. She'd lived in fear for too long.

While the tech set up his equipment to check her phone for a possible tracking device, the enormity of what had taken place there today finally sank in. She desperately needed a moment alone.

She rose to her feet. "I could use some coffee. Would anyone else like some?"

Both men nodded in unison.

"Let me help you," JT offered.

"No, it's okay…I can get it. I'll be right back." She hurried away before he could say anything else.

The kitchen was empty although several officers worked outside. For the time being, she was safe. Her stalker surely wouldn't try anything with so many law enforcement personnel around. Releasing a slow, steady breath, Faith got out the coffee supplies, and went about making a fresh pot.

As she waited for coffee to brew, she struggled to make sense of the shadowy images coming more frequently.

Since she'd stopped taking the meds prescribed for her at the hospital, things were becoming clearer. At times, she could almost see his face.

Her fingers shook as she poured the coffee into three cups.

"How are you holding up?" JT asked from the doorway. She hadn't heard him come in.

It took longer than she wished to steady her voice. "I'm fine. Did the tech find anything?"

JT shook his head. "No. He did a thorough sweep. There's no tracking device on the phone."

She sighed impatiently. "Then how does he keep finding me?"

"I don't know."

JT came into the room, took the cups from her and set them on the counter. He was so close. She could feel his warm breath against her face. His thumb stroked her cheek and she closed her eyes. She liked having him near, feeling his touch. Leaning on his strength.

"I know this is hard," he said gently.

It *was* hard, but having him in her corner made it so much easier. "Yes, but I'm all right...I'll be all right."

He grinned at her. "Ready?"

She was. She was ready to move beyond the darkness of the past two years. Ready for some happiness in her life.

JT picked up the cups and she trailed behind him to the great room.

"Thanks." Will accepted the coffee from JT, then he nodded at Faith. "I won't lie, the fact that we hit a dead end with the tracking device was a setback, but there has to be *some* way this guy keeps finding you. It took some doing, but I was able to put a trace on your cell phone right away. When he calls again we'll be ready for him."

"Let's hope he calls," JT told them grimly. "Because right now, nothing about this guy fits with what I've read about stalkers."

"I have to agree." Will's tone was tense. "I've worked dozens of stalking cases and there is always a history of some type. A love affair gone bad. Advances spurned by the victim. In cases not involving celebrities, I've never heard of someone stalking a person without having some unrequited interest in them. Unfortunately, your inability to remember your past puts us at a disadvantage. We don't know what we're up against."

His gaze bore into hers. She had a feeling he knew she hadn't told him everything.

"I know this has been hard for you, and I hate to be the bearer of more bad news, but I need you to understand something. This is going to get a whole lot worse before it gets better." Will didn't try to sugarcoat his words. "I can tell you one thing with absolute confidence—once this guy feels cornered, the violence will continue to escalate. We do have a slight edge, though. We know it's coming and there are things you can do to protect yourself."

He gave her a moment to process what he'd said.

"Such as?" Faith asked.

"For starters, I don't want you to leave the house. If you need something, ask for it. We'll get it for you."

She'd given up so much of her life already. Now she had to become a prisoner in her own home? How much more freedom did she have to relinquish?

"I've put my best officers on the house, but I'm going to suggest something as a precaution. JT, can you show her the proper way to use a weapon? At this point, we can't afford to be too careful. I'd rather you know how to take care of yourself just in case."

Faith struggled to collect her thoughts. This was really happening. She'd chosen to stop running and fight. There was no turning back now.

FOUR

"Can I talk to you for a second?" Will asked.

JT could tell from the inflection in his friend's voice there was something he wanted to tell him in private. "Sure." He turned to Faith. "I'll be right back."

"Okay," she said and closed her eyes. She looked ready to drop. Rehashing the details of her attack had taken its toll.

JT shut the door quietly and followed Will back to the kitchen.

"I didn't want to say this in front of Faith, but I won't be able to keep my officers here indefinitely. Let's hope we can figure out who's doing this soon, otherwise…" Will threw up his hands. "We're short-staffed as it is. I heard a little while ago they've just upgraded Tropical Storm Tyler to a hurricane and it appears to be heading right for us. If it stays on course, it should reach landfall by late Tuesday evening or possibly Wednesday morning, and we could be facing an all-out evacuation of the island."

JT let out a low whistle. That meant they had two days to figure out who was stalking Faith.

Will concentrated on the activity going on outside the kitchen window. "She hasn't told us everything. Any police officer worth his badge would have taken a complaint from an assault victim very seriously. Something doesn't add up."

JT had thought the same thing. "You're right. She's holding something back."

"She trusts you, JT. You need to get her to open up. Find out what she's keeping from us." He rubbed a hand across his face. "This guy's had a two-year head start on us, and the clock's ticking. We need to know the whole story and soon."

JT shrugged. "I'll do my best. I've asked Derek to check into her past to see what he can find out." Will shot him a surprised look. "Call it a gut feeling, but when I brought her dog back last night, I could see that she was terrified of something."

"Good idea. I'll do what I can to help, but we don't have much to go on and I can't tie up the additional manpower for long with what we do have." Will pointed toward the window. "We're about done here. I've ordered the truck towed to the police impound lot. We'll continue going over it, but I don't think we'll find anything."

JT clasped the chief's hand. "Thanks. I know this is the last thing you need right now, but I appreciate your help."

"No problem. We'll monitor her cell. Undoubtedly, he'll keep calling."

JT groaned when he spotted his sister's battered, old VW Bug pull into the driveway out front. Liz's arrival didn't surprise him much. As a former Hope Island police officer, Liz still monitored most of the calls coming over the police scanner and she was up very early every morning to see her husband Sam, a local fisherman, off to work. His sister had probably been on her second pot of coffee when the call came in.

Will noticed Liz a second later. "You're in trouble now.

She's found out you're part of this. She's going to want to know what's going on. I think that's my cue to leave."

Liz swung open the front door and stepped inside. She located her brother right away and ignored Will's "Good morning" entirely.

"Are you all right?" she asked as she rushed to his side. At almost six feet tall, blonde and physically fit, Liz had a way of capturing attention whenever she entered a room.

Today, she'd pulled her honey-blond hair up into a make-shift ponytail and thrown a jacket over her gray sweatpants and T-shirt. JT couldn't help but chuckle at his big sister's concern, even though at times she made him feel as if he were still ten years old instead of a thirty-three-year-old, successful businessman.

"I'm fine, Liz. What are you doing here?"

Her blue eyes filled with worry. "I heard the distress call go out for this address. I got in touch with Terry and he told me you called it in. What on earth happened? Are you all right?"

The last thing he needed right now was to try to explain the situation to Liz. "I'm fine. You didn't need to make a trip over here."

She arched one perfectly manicured brow at him. Liz always could see right through his bunk. "Don't be ridiculous, brother. You are not talking to a rookie. Something big happened here this morning. There wouldn't be this much police presence if it were nothing."

Will rolled his eyes, waved and stepped outside. JT watched as his friend got into his car and left.

There was a time before Ellie's birth and his sister's subsequent decision to quit the force that Liz had been next in line to take over Will's current position as chief of police. It had been a hard decision, but one Liz had never once regretted. Still, she enjoyed keeping up with the happenings of the island by listening to the police scanner. She probably knew more about the island then JT did.

"Someone took a couple of shots at me." Liz's mouth flew open. "But I'm fine," he quickly reassured her. "Faith, the house's new tenant, called me when she thought she had a prowler. When I got here, someone started firing shots off. We're still trying to figure out what's going on."

"Good grief. You could have been killed! What kind of trouble is this woman in?"

Close by, someone cleared their throat. JT and Liz both turned and spotted Faith standing in the kitchen doorway. Neither of them had heard her come in. He could only imagine how she'd taken Liz's comments. His sister at least had the good grace to appear embarrassed. In spite of Liz's impetuous tongue, she was one of the kindest people he knew.

All the fight went out of Liz and she went over to Faith and extended her hand. "I'm sorry. That was a terrible thing to say and none of my business. JT is always telling me I'm overprotective. I'm Liz Richards, by the way. JT's sister."

After a slight hesitation, Faith took her hand. "Faith McKenzie."

Liz gave her a sympathetic smile. "JT told me what happened. How terrifying. Do you have any idea who might have done this?"

Just like his sister to cut straight to the heart of the matter. "Liz…" But it didn't matter, Faith wasn't listening. She was staring at Liz's locket.

"Is something wrong?" he asked.

Faith looked as if she'd just seen something frightening before she shook her head. "No, it's nothing." Even so, her voice came out strained.

Liz glanced around the enormous kitchen and at the

disarray of someone who hadn't unpacked. "This house is wonderful, isn't it? I always loved the kitchen, but it's so big. Are you still settling in okay?"

Faith blushed slightly. "Um, yes, I guess. I'm still trying to find the right place for everything." Of course, Liz knew Faith had been renting the house for a month. She'd been the one to tell JT about his new neighbor. His sister was picking up on all the same signs he'd noticed the day before.

"I see." Clearly she didn't. Liz was all about organization. "Well, if you need any help, I'm available most days. I should warn you, though. I'm good at minimalizing. My poor husband is scared to death I'm going to throw away something he needs one day."

Faith actually smiled then. "Thank you. I might take you up on your offer."

"Good. Oh, and when you're ready, I'd be happy to show you around Hope Island. The city council renovated the downtown district a few years back. There are some nice shops and a great seafood restaurant. We could have lunch whenever you want."

"I'd like that."

Liz started to say something more when JT interrupted her. "Time to go." Faith had been through enough without any more of his sister's interrogations.

"JT," his sister protested as he ushered her to the door.

"Later, Liz. I promise we'll talk later."

JT closed the door on his sister's protests and came back to Faith. "Sorry. She means well, but sometimes she doesn't know when to quit. How are you holding up?"

Truth be told, the reality of what Liz had said brought home the truth and scared her to death. "I'm fine, but she's right, you know. I had no business calling you, JT. You could have been killed."

He reached out, clasping her hand in his. "Hey, I'm fine and I can take care of myself. Stop worrying."

The heat of his touch made it suddenly hard to draw air into her lungs. Her heart hammered her chest as if she'd run a marathon. She could feel her misgivings crumbling.

Something shifted in his eyes as they held hers. "I think I'll make some more coffee…" he said absently as if it were hard to keep his thoughts together. "Would you like some?"

At first, the shrilling phone seemed disjointed. Unreal. As if part of the nightmare had found its way into a sweet dream. JT stared at her as unwelcome reality intruded between them.

He abruptly let her go, grabbed the phone from the counter and handed it to her. "Put it on speaker and try to keep him on the line as long as you can."

Her fingers shook as she took the phone. She did as he asked and the familiar song filled the tense silence of the room. Time slowed to a crawl and then…he spoke.

"You shouldn't have gone to the police. You made a dreadful mistake. Now you're going to have to pay. It's your turn to die."

The phone slipped from her hand and clattered against the floor. *He spoke.* Her mind reeled. He'd never uttered a word before. Faith drew in handfuls of air to keep from hyperventilating.

JT retrieved the phone from where it fell. "Hello? Hello, is anyone there?" With no answer, he dropped the phone on the counter. She could tell from his taut expression that the connection hadn't lasted long enough to trace the call.

He took out his phone and quickly punched in a number. "He just called. Did you get it?" he asked, his eyes glued to Faith. "Right. That's what I thought. I'll call you if anything new happens here." JT disconnected the call.

"Another dead end?"

"Afraid so. My guess is now that he knows the police are involved this will be the last time we hear from him... by phone." He didn't say as much but she knew. Her stalker was no longer toying with her.

"What aren't you telling us, Faith? There has to be more to the story than what you told Will and me earlier." She started to deny it but he wouldn't let her. "I need the truth. All of it. And I need it now." Frustration lent a hard edge to his voice.

Her hand went automatically up to tug at her top in an effort to hide the scar but he stopped her. His fingers gently pulled the collar away to reveal a raised red scar. "Please, just tell me."

She sank down onto one of the barstools close by. "I was attacked. That much is true, but something else happened that night. Something horrible." She couldn't read anything from his expression. She took a deep breath and continued. "The night of my assault, two people, my best friend and her father, were murdered."

Shock filled his expression. "That's...terrible. What happened?" JT prompted when it was hard for her to keep going. Every time she thought about that night, what Rachel and Carl must have gone through, the guilt became staggering. Why had she been the one to live while they had to die? What did he want from her?

JT pulled out the stool next to hers. He was waiting for answers and she knew she desperately needed his help, but could she really tell another living soul all those appalling things?

The tenderness she saw in him helped her go on. "I

don't know much about what happened. Just what I was told after the attack."

"Okay," he said gently. "Did the police have any idea what happened?"

Her hands shook and she clasped them together in her lap. "The police thought it started as a simple home invasion then something went wrong. He killed Rachel and her father right away. One theory is that I may have been in another part of the house at the time and the killer didn't realize it…or maybe I tried to get away and he caught me. All I know is two innocent people died that night."

JT thought about what she'd said. "I'm guessing something must have happened to distract him."

"I assume so. At least that's what the police believed. What I don't understand is why Rachel and Carl were killed and I wasn't. After he committed the murders, the killer set a fire to destroy evidence inside the house, but when the cops found me, I was outside and some distance from the house. I guess that after he attacked me I tried to escape, but if he took the time to set a fire, then why not take care of the only witness left who could place him at the scene?"

The thought of what Rachel's and Carl's final moments must have been like haunted her every day she lived and they didn't.

"You're right, it doesn't make sense. Even if something or someone did interrupt him, letting you live was a liability he couldn't afford. You obviously saw his face. When you said that no one was ever charged with the stalking, I take it no one was ever charged with their murders, either? What about suspects? Did the police like anyone for the murders?"

She had no idea if the police liked anyone for the murders. Every time she asked for information on the case, the police shut her down. They'd been less than forthcoming with the facts as well. It had taken weeks before she'd even learned the details of the fire.

"As far as I know, they never had anyone in mind."

"So why did the police believe it might have been part of a home invasion?"

"Apparently there had been a string of home invasions around the area at the time."

"Was anything reported missing from the Jennings' house?"

"That's the part that never made sense. If the person responsible for the crime went to such extremes as to take the lives of two people, then why not finish the job and rob the place? But according to Rachel's cousin, nothing was reported stolen."

"Rachel's cousin?" JT prompted.

"Ben Jennings. He's the one who went through the house once it was cleared and told the police nothing appeared to be missing."

"Did he live there?"

She remembered Ben had told her once he had an apartment downtown. "No."

"Then how would he know if anything had been taken?"

"I think he stayed at the ranch quite often. I spoke with him shortly after the social worker took me home from the hospital. Their deaths were devastating for him."

"We need to talk to him. See what he remembers. He might be able to shed some light on what happened. At least give us another perspective. How well do you know him?"

"We talked several times on the phone, but I never met him in person. I was still in the hospital at the time of Rachel's and Carl's funerals. Ben is very nice and I'm sure he'd be willing to do whatever he could to help solve his family's murders." She still remembered those calls as if they were yesterday. Ben had wept over the loss of his family, and his outpouring of grief had left an indelible mark on her. She'd felt so helpless. If only she could remember something.

"Did the police give you any indication as to why they didn't think the calls were connected to the murders?"

She shook her head. "Like I said, they acted like I made the whole thing up." She wasn't being totally upfront with JT. She hated talking about the detectives' innuendos. At first, they'd only hinted at the possibility of her involvement in what had happened to the Jennings. Later on, those hints had turned into accusations. The only reason they'd let her go was the lack of evidence against her. She'd lost her friends, her memory, her sense of security, and she'd been terrified she would lose her freedom as well.

"I don't get it. With everything that happened to you, you'd think they would have investigated the calls more thoroughly." He thought about it for a minute and then asked, "What about Carl Jennings and his daughter? Was there any indication they may have been having trouble with someone prior to their deaths?"

Faith had gone over every possible scenario in her head a thousand times. Researched Rachel and Carl online, yet nothing out of the ordinary appeared to be happening in their lives. Certainly nothing that would have prompted someone to murder them. "No. Everyone loved them."

JT ran a jerky hand through his hair. "What about Carl's business dealings? Anything unusual there? I'm thinking maybe one of his business deals put him in contact with someone dangerous."

She didn't believe it for a second. Everything she'd uncovered about Carl Jennings indicated he was a well-respected businessman.

The most surprising piece of information she'd learned about him had actually come from the police. Even though she couldn't remember anything about it, they told her she had worked for Carl as his accountant shortly before his death.

Faith struggled to let go of those ugly memories. "Carl was a real estate developer at the time of his death, but his family made a fortune in oil before he sold the business after his son, who was a few years older than Rachel, was killed in an explosion on one of his rigs. At the time, the Jennings family lived in Midland. After Carl quit the oil business, he bought the ranch outside of Austin and started developing commercial real estate a few years later. Carl was responsible for building some of the most desirable shopping centers and hotels in Austin and—"

She stopped midsentence. How did she know about Carl's son dying? She couldn't recall the police ever mentioning it. Had Rachel told her about her brother's death or had she simply read it somewhere? She tried to remember the news reports concerning the Jennings family. There had been something mentioned about Carl's son, but nothing about how he'd died.

"What is it?" JT had seen her hesitate.

She shook her head. "Nothing." What if those memories had nothing to do with Carl Jennings's past? Maybe she'd become so desperate she was conjuring up false memories.

JT covered her hand with his. His calloused thumb stroked over her fingers. She swallowed hard but the lump in her throat just wouldn't go away.

When she met his eyes she forgot about the danger she faced. The troubled past she couldn't remember. Awareness sparked between them again and for a second she thought he might kiss her.

He cleared his throat. "Thank you for telling me. I know

it must be difficult to rehash those terrible memories, but now that you have, a lot of things make sense. I understand now why you've been so terrified."

She struggled to achieve the same level of calm he'd found. "The doctors kept telling me my memory should return in time. I was even prescribed medication to help, but it didn't."

Something she said got his attention. "Wait...what type of medication did they prescribe? Do you still have the bottle?"

"Yes. They're upstairs in my bathroom. The drug is called Zyban, but I stopped taking the pills last week because they weren't helping. In fact, they seemed to make things worse. I couldn't concentrate or think clearly."

She could tell the name of the drug didn't ring any bells for him. "Who prescribed them?"

"The doctor who treated me at the hospital, Alex Stephens. Why? Is that important?"

"Maybe. I'm not sure. I'll check it out. At this point, we can't afford to dismiss anything. How did you get the prescription refilled when you moved around so much?"

"Online. I ordered the prescription through a website. They arrived in the mail every couple of months."

"For two years? Wouldn't the prescription have to be refilled by then? Did you contact the doctor?"

She looked over at him and shrugged. "To be honest, I never really thought about it until now. Dr. Stephens always managed to have the prescription renewed for me before it ran out. I was just grateful that he was being so diligent."

"That is odd. Most doctors would insist on seeing a patient before they refilled a prescription after so long. At the very least they'd have you check in with a local doctor."

JT was right—it didn't make sense. "I'll go get them for you." Faith ran upstairs and grabbed the bottle from her medicine cabinet. Less than a handful of the pills remained.

She handed them to JT once she returned to the kitchen.

"Thanks." He examined the bottle for a second then stuck them in his pocket. "I take it since the night of the attack, nothing from your past has returned?"

She started to answer no, but then bit her lip.

"What is it?" he prompted.

"I'm not sure. It may be nothing, but there was something familiar about the roses and I've been trying to figure out what. I think at one time, they may have been my favorite flower, but something changed that. And what I told you about Carl selling the oil business after his son died on one of his rigs? That was never published anywhere. The papers simply mentioned he'd sold a successful business in Midland and started his own real estate development business a few years before his death. Then today, when Liz was here, I noticed the locket she wore around her neck…"

JT appeared lost for a second. "Oh, right. Sam gave her the locket when Ellie was born."

Faith remembered JT mentioning his niece before. It was easy to see he adored the child. She was drawn to JT's strong sense of family. For someone with no family connection, she yearned for it. "When I saw it, I remembered…something. I don't know if it's real or just something I've imagined."

"I know this is hard." His eyes met hers and she forgot what she'd been about to say. His expression grew serious and he reached out and tucked a strand of hair behind her ear. "Are you up to trying something?"

She agreed with a shake of her head because forming words was hard to do.

He smiled gently. "Good. I don't want you to try to

analyze what you're about to say, just tell me what you remembered."

She closed her eyes against the disturbing distraction JT represented. However, he didn't seem to suffer from the roller-coaster ride of emotions that she did. Had she imagined this attraction between them? "I think it was my sixteenth birthday. My father gave me a locket similar to the one Liz wore. It had a photo of my mother in it."

"It's something, anyway," JT said.

She opened her eyes and stared at him. "But that's just it. My parents died when I was a child. That memory couldn't be mine."

"That's a very detailed memory to not have some importance in your life, even if it's not exactly as you recalled it. It could mean you're regaining your memory and it's definitely something to go on. I take it these are the first ones that have come back to you?"

She desperately hoped JT was right. "Yes. Everything else is still blank. You have no idea how frightening not remembering who you are can be."

"Tell me what it's been like," he prodded gently.

"Well, before the hospital would discharge me, they were trying to find a relative or friend, someone who could check in on me from time to time, but there wasn't anyone. The social worker they assigned to me was very nice. She took me home and made sure I had food in the apartment." Her voice shook and she fought back tears of frustration. "But I'll never forget how surreal it felt when I stepped through the door for the first time. I knew this was where I lived, and yet nothing was familiar."

JT shook his head. "I can't even imagine. I'm sorry you've had to go through this."

In truth, the unknown had been paralyzing. She couldn't sleep. Couldn't leave her apartment. Couldn't banish the fear no matter how many lights she turned on. She'd become a prisoner to it.

"What was your life like after that?" JT asked.

"I felt as if I lived in a country where I didn't speak the language. Everything was foreign. There were very few personal items in the apartment for me to get any real sense of what my life was like. I found a couple of photos taken of Rachel and me but little else. It was almost as if I hadn't existed before."

"You must have been terrified. And then, a week later, when those phone calls started coming..." There was a long pause. "You said the guy's never spoken until tonight?"

"That's right."

"Did you recognize his voice?"

If only it were that easy. "No. I've never heard it before. His voice sounded muffled on the phone."

JT's mouth tightened. "I'm not really surprised. Apparently, he was trying to disguise his voice by holding a cloth over the mouthpiece, which tells me you probably do know him."

What little bit of hope she'd been holding on to evaporated into thin air when she saw the truth in JT's eyes. He was a professional. He'd seen dozens of similar cases. She knew she could never run far or fast enough to escape the person stalking her. One way or another, one of them was going to die.

Bit by bit, as JT listened to Faith's story, the facts about the case proved his initial theory to be correct. While this might have started as a stalking case, something changed along the way, and then culminated in two murders. What didn't make sense was why the killer hadn't taken Faith's life that night. Perhaps the guy had an infatuation with

Faith that prevented him from killing her. Or it could be something else entirely. All JT knew for certain was that, up until now, the stalker had been content to manipulate her through fear into doing his will. This seemed to indicate the perpetrator knew about Faith's memory loss and wanted to keep it that way.

But JT's and the police's involvement had been a game changer. If she regained her memory, she could identify the killer. Still, JT had a feeling there was something more to the story. What piece of information did Faith have locked away in her memory that had cost two people their lives?

He made a mental note to have Derek check into the medication prescribed to Faith. Something about that didn't add up, either.

Shoving his thoughts aside, he looked into Faith's troubled blue eyes. "I'll call Will. Let him know everything you told me. It should be a tremendous help. I'm also calling in my security team. They're the best when it comes to finding information others have missed." JT's heart went out to her. She had lived through years of torment and it wasn't close to being over. He had a feeling they were in for some rough days ahead.

"I'm not sure what good any of this will do," she told him in a flat tone. "The case is still open and the police haven't exactly been cooperative. How do you plan to get them to give you key information on an unsolved murder case?"

She was right. It wouldn't be easy. "Let us worry about that. If anyone can get the information, Will can. I just need you not to give up. This could take some time."

The hope in her eyes scared him to death. She trusted everything to him. He couldn't let her down.

"I promise, but only if you agree to one thing."

He was curious. "Anything."

"If you find out something…no matter *what* you find out, whether it's good or bad, you'll tell me about it."

He squeezed her hand then pulled her to her feet. "I promise. No matter what I discover, I'll tell you everything."

JT decided Faith had been through enough for one day. She needed to rest. "I'm going home for a bit to shower and take care of some business. I'll let the officers outside know I'm leaving. If it's okay with you, I'd like to take your phone with me on the off chance he calls again." JT took out his phone and handed it to her. "Here, keep mine with you. If you need me, call my home number."

She nodded and walked him to the door. "Lock up behind me." He leaned close and stroked her cheek. "Try not to worry. You're safe."

He waited until all three of the locks engaged before heading over to the police car parked a little ways from the house. JT hadn't wanted her to see, but all his old doubts had resurfaced. What if he'd made her a promise he couldn't fulfill? He hadn't been able to save Emily. What made him think he could save Faith?

Outside, dark gray clouds gathered low on the ocean. A light mist had begun to fall and the waves slammed against the shore with renewed anger.

"Everything okay?" JT leaned in the driver's side window. He knew both officers from his days on the force. Will had chosen two of his best.

"Been quiet out here," the driver, Officer Samuels, said.

"Good. Let's hope it stays that way. I'm heading home for a little while. I'll stop by later this evening." Samuels gave him a two-finger salute and JT started back behind the house in the direction of the beach.

The late-October breeze held a touch of the coming winter in it. Most of the tourists had left the island already. Before they knew it, snow would blanket the island and then it would be empty of everyone except the people who called Hope Island home. This was his favorite time of year. No traffic jams. No crowded stores. Just a quiet solitude that helped him slow his chaotic life down and catch up on some simple things he loved doing, like fixing up his house.

JT unlocked the door and barely made it inside when Liz called. He wondered how many times she'd tried to reach him before resorting to calling his home phone. He'd put his cell phone on vibrate so that he could concentrate on what Faith said and now she had his phone. His sister must be going out of her mind with worry. He glanced at his watch. He couldn't believe it was already nine o'clock. The morning had been a blur.

"What, are you spying on me now?" He tried to infuse some humor into his tone.

Liz's laugh sounded halfhearted. "No. I'm just worried. Why aren't you answering your cell?"

Her call didn't surprise him. After all, he'd given her plenty of reason to worry in the past. "I left it at Faith's. I'm fine, so stop worrying."

"I can't help it, you're still my baby brother. Have you listened to the weather report lately? The hurricane is definitely coming our way. Sam and I are thinking of taking Ellie to his sister's for a few days after we get the house storm proofed. You should come with us."

He loved his sister's concern, but they both knew he wasn't going with her. "That's a good idea. You go. I can't leave right now."

"JT…"

"Liz, stop worrying." Outside, the wind pelted rain against the window.

"Someone tried to kill you today, JT. You don't even

know who or what you're dealing with. I have a bad feeling about all this. I couldn't bear it if anything happened to you."

She was thinking about Emily's death. The two had been best friends most of their lives. Liz had been devastated when Emily died. It had made her cling tighter to her brother.

"I'll be all right. Take Ellie away for a few days and try not to worry about me. When the governor issues the evacuation order, I'll leave the island." He knew he was wasting his time telling her not to worry.

Liz groaned loudly. "Okay, but you'd better keep in touch. I want to know you're safe."

He chuckled at his sister's attempt at bullying him. "I promise I'll do my best. I love you, sis. Take care of Sam and Ellie."

JT hung up the phone and clicked on the TV. The local station had begun advising residents of nearby islands to evacuate.

"The governor is expected to issue evacuation orders for Hatton and Sophia Island soon with orders for Hope Island expected to follow if the storm remains on its current path. The outer edge of Hurricane Tyler should make landfall at Hatton Island sometime late Monday into early Tuesday morning. The storm is expected to reach Hope Island late Tuesday night or Wednesday morning. Here's what you need to do to be prepared..."

They had roughly two days to figure out who wanted Faith dead before they had to evacuate the island.

JT muted the volume and called Will. "You were right. There is more to Faith's story than she initially told us. A lot more." He ran through the details of what he'd found out about the Jennings murders.

"This puts the case in a completely different league.

We're not just dealing with someone who's unhinged. We're facing someone who's unhinged and not afraid to commit murder. Up until this point, he's kept her alive for a reason. We need to figure out what that reason is."

"Which won't be easy." JT sighed. With Faith unable to remember crucial pieces of what happened the night of the attack, finding out the identity of the killer would be next to impossible.

"I agree."

It felt as if the perfect storm was in the works with the hurricane bearing down on them and a killer stalking his prey. The only question was how many casualties there would be once it was all said and done.

"How's Faith holding up?" Will asked.

"Okay, I guess. Considering." JT hesitated then asked, "Do you have any contacts on the Austin force?"

Will picked up right away on where JT was going with this. "You want me to get the police records of the Jennings case for you."

"Yes."

"I'll make it happen somehow," Will assured him.

"Thanks. I can't tell you how much I appreciate your help with this."

Will's lengthy silence had JT thinking he wasn't going to like what was coming next. "JT, you're my friend and you know I'll do anything to help you, but you understand how serious this is, right? This person is very dangerous and until we know who he is, we're working in the dark. He could be anybody."

JT understood Will had his best interests at heart. "I realize that, but—"

"Just hear me out for a second," Will interrupted. "I know how difficult getting through Emily's death was for you, but it doesn't matter how many people you try to save, you can't bring her back."

JT closed his eyes. Of course, his friend was right. After Emily's death, he'd been plagued by guilt. It had caused him to quit the force completely. He knew if he ever was going to move forward, he had to find a way to deal with the guilt, so he'd formed Wyatt Securities. In a way, he was like Faith. They were both stuck in the past.

"Losing Emily shook your faith in a lot of things—God included—but it's time you forgave yourself. It wasn't your fault."

JT swallowed back emotions that were always just below the surface whenever he thought about his late wife. "You're wrong. I should have been the one to go into the store that night. I should have been the one who died. Instead, I was tired and didn't want to mess with it." Nausea roiled in his gut, but he forced the words out. "I let Emily walk into a robbery and I lost my wife because of it. I *need* to do this, Will. I need to feel like I'm helping save someone's life to make up for letting Emily down."

"And what happens if you can't save Faith? We both know that's a real possibility. What then?"

To that, JT had no answer.

"Is there something more going on between you two?" his friend asked quietly.

The no-holds-barred directness of Will's question prompted JT to examine his motives closely. He couldn't deny he was attracted to Faith, but what he felt for her went beyond a physical fascination. Would it lead to anything? He wasn't sure. Did he want it to? For the first time since Emily's death, he believed he might be ready to move on.

"I'm just trying to help someone in need, but you're right about one thing. I did lose faith in a lot of things, including God. I think He put Faith in my life for a reason. Maybe I need her help as much as she needs mine."

"All right," Will said at last. "You know what you're doing. It's just I haven't seen you look at a woman the way you look at Faith in a long time."

Seconds ticked by while JT tried to deny it and couldn't.

Will chuckled softly. "I guess that answers my question. I'm praying for you. For both of you."

FIVE

An explosion rocketed through the house, rattling windows and shaking the furniture. Faith shot up in bed just as the alarm's siren split the quiet and her heartbeat thudded in her chest.

Was she dreaming? Had the blast been real or part of a dream? As the alarm continued to blare, Faith realized this was no dream. Someone was trying to break into the house.

She hadn't meant to fall asleep. She'd just wanted to rest for a second, but exhaustion had taken over and she'd fallen asleep the second her head hit the pillow with Ollie close by her side.

She glanced around the dark room. The Pug was nowhere in sight and something was terribly wrong. She couldn't breathe.

Faith drew in a handful of deep breaths and started to cough. The air tasted bitter. Acrid. Tears streamed from her eyes. It was impossible to see more than a few feet in front of her as smoke poured into the room.

The house was on fire.

She hurled her body out of bed and kept low to the floor. Faith grabbed the first thing her fingers came in contact with, a scarf lying on the chair near the bed. She wrapped it around her nose and mouth and crawled toward the door.

"Ollie," Faith called out and choked on the smoke. The closer she got to the door the heavier it became.

Dear God, please don't let us be trapped.

Once she reached the door, she realized she'd left it cracked open. That's how the dog must have gotten out.

"Ollie, where are you?" She wouldn't leave without her beloved pet. He'd been with her through some of the worst moments in her life.

She listened and heard a faint whimpering coming from the landing of the stairs. Ollie...

Before she could call the dog again, she heard it. Glass breaking downstairs. It sounded like it came from the back of the house. She couldn't move, her body frozen with fear. "Please help me. Please don't let me die like this." She whispered the prayer into the smoke-filled room. As if in answer, Ollie squeezed through the narrow opening in the door and jumped into her arms, licking her face. Faith closed the door as quietly as she could and then crawled underneath the bed.

"Shh," she whispered against Ollie's ear, and the dog seemed to understand the urgency. He buried his head against her chest.

She could feel the Pug shaking in her arms. Ollie was scared to death. It dawned on her the alarm had stopped blaring. Had he somehow disabled it? She had been so terrified by the fire and so desperate to find Ollie that she hadn't noticed the silence until now. The only noise was the fire and footsteps moving around downstairs.

With her heart beating a frantic pace against her chest, Faith closed her eyes. *Let not your heart be troubled...* She recited her favorite verse over and over in her head. God was in control. No matter what happened, she'd trust Him to see her through this nightmare.

A sense of calm slipped over her. She opened her eyes and listened. A door slammed somewhere downstairs. She could no longer hear the footsteps. The only sound in the house was the fire raging. She knew if she wanted to live, she had to get herself and Ollie out as quickly as possible, before the dense smoke pouring into the room took the choice away from them.

Without any moonlight and with the rain continuing to fall, the area of beach leading to Faith's place seemed even more isolated than usual. JT had made a judgment call and had chosen to walk back to her house instead of taking the Suburban. He hoped it had been the right move because right now he wasn't so sure. Before he reached the stretch of beach behind Faith's house, he heard it. An explosion. It sounded as if someone had detonated a small bomb.

JT reached for his phone then remembered he'd forgotten Faith's phone at his house.

He sprinted toward the now-burning house, his heartbeat mirroring his footsteps. The entire kitchen area appeared to be missing. Flames licked out through a gaping hole.

The fire had rendered the back of the house inaccessible. He skirted the side and cleared the top step of the porch in a single move.

"Faith." He called out her name as he tried the front door and found it unlocked. The second he opened it, smoke blasted him. He choked and covered his mouth with his arm. He could hardly see anything as he entered the house.

"Faith!" The fire had completely engulfed the kitchen by now, and time was running out. He frantically searched the rooms downstairs, all the while shouting out her name.

He'd started up the stairs when he heard it. A whimpering sound. He stopped and listened. Ollie. It was coming from Faith's bedroom.

JT took the steps two at a time. "Faith!"

"I'm in here," she called out. JT raced for the door just as she opened it.

"Come on. We have to get out of here now." He hurried back down the stairs with Faith following close behind him. So far, the fire seemed confined to the kitchen and laundry area.

They reached the front door and he cracked it and stopped. "Stay here until I make sure he's not out there waiting for us."

He stepped outside and drew his weapon. He said a quick prayer and left the porch. JT glanced around the area. It was pitch-black and the rain made it next to impossible to see anything. If the killer were still on the property, they'd be sitting ducks, but he had to get Faith out of the house before the whole place went up in flames.

Why hadn't the two officers watching the house come to Faith's rescue? He didn't like it. He couldn't see any movement coming from the car.

JT raced up the steps and grabbed Faith's hand. "I can't see anything and the two officers watching the house aren't moving. We need to make it to the trees behind the house. He won't be able to see us from there."

He pulled her along behind him until they reached a clump of trees separating her property line from the beach.

Faith jerked the scarf from her face. She leaned over and put her hand on her knees, coughing and trying to draw enough air into her lungs.

"I need you to wait here. I'm going to check on the officers. They should have reacted to the explosion by now. Something's wrong."

She clutched his arm in a death grip. "I'm coming with you. I don't want to stay here alone." The determination in her eyes made it impossible to refuse. She was the target and he needed to protect her, yet he understood her fear and he didn't like leaving her alone.

"Okay, but stay close."

He held out his hand and she took it and followed him. He could feel her soft breath against his neck.

JT stopped when they reached the tree line. Flames had completely engulfed the downstairs of the house by now. The rain at least helped to keep the fire from spreading at a faster rate, but the strength of the wind worked against them. It licked flames in all directions. He needed to call the fire in. He reached for his cell phone and realized it was still in the house and he'd left Faith's at his place.

Had something happened to the two officers? Was that why they hadn't responded to the fire? An uneasy feeling slipped into the pit of his stomach. This didn't bode well. The patrol car was some twenty feet in front of them and already he could see the glass was missing from the driver's-side door. If the killer were close, the minute they cleared the trees they'd be an easy target, but he couldn't leave without checking on the two men in the car.

He and Faith left the protection of the trees and moved cautiously toward the back of the vehicle. Still no one moved inside the car.

JT stopped. "Get down and wait here. I need to check it out first." She didn't answer but did as he asked.

He edged toward the driver's side. That window was shattered and so was the one on the passenger side. Someone had shot them out. Shards of glass still clung to the door. The killer had probably used the same weapon as the one he'd fired on JT. Rain dripped through the opening in the window onto Samuels's face. He lay slumped in the seat at an awkward angle, half leaning against the door.

Blood oozed from a multitude of gunshot wounds. Even before JT tried to find a pulse, he knew there was no way anyone could survive such a brutal attack. Kennedy was dead as well. The killer had ripped the radio transponder from the machine. JT searched for their cell phones. They were missing. The killer had murdered two police officers in cold blood before setting the fire. And he could still be out there now, waiting for the right moment to…

"Run," JT yelled as he reached Faith's side and grabbed her hand, dragging her with him. When they reached the trees once more, he stopped long enough for them to catch their breath.

She jerked her hand free. "We have to go back. We have to help them," she shouted over the noise of the flames and the ocean. He could see that she was crying.

"They're dead, Faith. We can't help them. Whoever killed those two officers is probably watching us. We can't stop…we have to keep going."

While the trees afforded a small amount of protection from the elements, every time he breathed out he could see his breath. With nightfall, the temperature had dropped considerably. If they stayed out here much longer, they'd be at risk of hyperthermia.

"Hang on a second." When they reached the beach, JT tugged her close as he listened for any indication they might have been followed, but he couldn't hear anything above the noise of the rain and the ocean. "Stay near the tree line and whatever you do don't let go of my hand," he whispered against her ear.

Covering the quarter-mile distance to his house seemed to take forever. He constantly checked back over his shoulder to make sure no one followed them. By the time they reached his back door, they were both soaked to the bone and shivering from the cold.

JT unlocked the door and they hurried inside. "I'll be right back," he told her after securing the dead bolt. He went to the closet and pulled out a couple of blankets. Faith still clutched Ollie tight, as if she were holding onto a lifeline. "Here. Put this around your shoulders. It'll help warm you up." He cranked up the heat and then grabbed his house phone to call the fire department. "This is JT Wyatt. There's a fire at 21 Ocean Way. I need you to send help right away."

Telling Will about the death of his two officers was one of the hardest things JT had ever had to do. Samuels and Kennedy were good men. Their families had lived on Hope Island for generations. The community, as well as the force, would feel their loss.

JT disconnected the call and turned to Faith. She was soaking wet and shaking uncontrollably. She was suffering from shock and probably the first stages of hyperthermia.

"We need to get you warmed up," he told her gently. "There's a shower upstairs you can use. I'll show you where it is."

She nodded and set Ollie on the floor.

When they reached the guest bedroom, he stopped. "Fresh towels are in the linen closet next to the shower. I think my sister left some clothes behind from when she and her family stayed here after their house flooded. They should fit you." He went over to a dresser, pulled out a set of gray sweats and handed them to her. "It's the best I can do. Go get warmed up and I'll see you downstairs in a few minutes."

He started to leave when her next words stopped him

in his tracks. "Those men. They're dead because of me. I don't know how to live with that."

Tears rimmed her eyes and his heart broke for her. "No. No, Faith. This isn't your fault." He came over to where she stood, then pulled her into his arms. "None of this is your fault. You can't take on the blame. That's what he wants you to think. Don't let him win."

She pulled away and tried to be strong. "I know that in my head, but it's so hard. I don't understand why he's doing any of this. What does he hope to gain?"

Another question he didn't know how to answer. "I'm not sure. I just think there's more to the story than we understand right now. I believe you know something he doesn't want made public."

She shook her head. "I don't have a clue what I could possibly know. I was an accountant. I didn't exactly have a lot of high-profile clients."

JT brushed back her wet hair from her face. "We'll figure it out together."

She desperately wanted to believe him. "Thank you."

"For what?" he asked softly.

"For believing me. For not thinking I'm crazy."

"Never. You're not crazy. What you've been through would have broken most people. You're a strong woman, Faith McKenzie. You just have to believe that yourself. I'll see you downstairs in a bit."

He didn't voice his thoughts aloud because he wanted her to keep fighting, but she was going to need every bit of strength she possessed to see this nightmare through to the end.

JT checked on Ollie then went into the great room and turned on the gas fireplace. Within a matter of minutes, the room was considerably warmer. Ollie followed him and began sniffing around.

As JT listened to the shower running upstairs, his thoughts reeled with possibilities. Why hadn't the killer finished the job after he murdered the officers? He certainly would have had the perfect chance unless something happened. Had he seen JT approaching and run off or did the alarm scare him? One thing was for sure—they were dealing with one very intelligent yet very disturbed individual.

With the amount of rainfall, he knew it was unlikely that Will's team would find any useful DNA at Faith's home. The attack on the officers had happened so suddenly JT doubted if Samuels and Kennedy had even known what hit them. The killer seemed to be gaining confidence with each new move he made.

JT glanced at his watch. Half an hour had passed since he'd notified Will about the officers' deaths. By now, Liz would know what had happened. He'd phone her before Faith came downstairs.

Liz picked up before the first ring ended. "JT. I was so worried when I heard the call over the police scanner."

He tried to keep his voice steady. No need to alarm her any more. "I'm okay. We're both okay. Things have been crazy."

"I heard. I can't believe it. Charlotte Samuels attended our Ladies' Bible Study yesterday. Eric Kennedy hasn't been married more than six months. He and Gen are still newlyweds."

JT understood exactly what those two men's families were going through. He'd been there. It was nothing short of a living nightmare.

"I'm scared for you, brother. What's happening in Faith's life for someone to go to such extremes?"

Upstairs, the shower was shut off. "I don't know."

"Please tell me you aren't thinking of taking her on as

a client? JT, I don't think that's a good idea. She's obviously in a lot of danger."

He'd expected Liz's reaction. "We haven't talked about it yet, but she needs my help, sis. Aren't you the one who's always telling me by helping others we help ourselves?"

He could tell from her silence she hadn't liked his answer. "Call me when you find out something. I'll be praying for you and for the officers' families."

It always humbled him to hear that his sister prayed for him. He wished he could find something to say to ease her mind, but he had no idea how this thing would end.

The warm spray of water helped to take the chill from her skin, but nothing could wash away the bitter cold growing inside her. The death count was growing. Four people were now dead and she was still no closer to understanding why.

Faith dressed in the sweats JT lent her and went downstairs, where she found him waiting for her in the great room. She noticed he'd changed into something dry as well. Ollie roamed around the room getting into things.

When the dog spotted her, he sprang into her arms.

Faith sat down on the sofa close to the fireplace. "Any word yet?" She dreaded his answer.

He shook his head. "No, nothing yet, but then I suspect they'll be at it for hours yet."

She stared into the fire. "JT, I was so afraid. The room filled with smoke and I couldn't breathe. Ollie had disappeared. Once I found him, I knew I had to get us out before the smoke became too overpowering. I started down the stairs, when I heard glass breaking and someone moving around downstairs." She released a quivering breath. "I thought he would kill me and then he just left. He must have heard you. If you hadn't showed up when you did…" She couldn't go on.

JT sat down beside her and reached for her hand. "So he went inside the house. I'm wondering if there might be some footprints we can use. Do you remember anything else?"

"Not really." She stopped. No, she did remember something. "Wait. There was a loud noise like an explosion. I thought it was part of my dream until the room filled with smoke."

JT remembered the explosion clearly. "I heard it, too. I'm guessing he used some kind of accelerant to set the fire. Possibly a firebomb."

It sounded terrifying. Once more JT had saved her life.

"I thought I noticed an alarm system before. Didn't that go off?" JT asked. "When I got there, it wasn't on."

"I remember hearing it, but not for long. Maybe a couple of minutes."

"Either the explosion took the security system out pretty quickly or the killer disabled it."

Her eyes widened as she remembered something. "Your phone. I left it on my nightstand."

"It's okay. I can get it when the fire chief clears the house again. In the meantime, if anyone needs me, they can call my home number."

She couldn't seem to stop shivering. "So what happens next?"

"I don't know. With your permission, I'd like to have two of my partners from Wyatt Securities start working the case. Like me, Teddy and Derek are former cops and they've been with me since the beginning. Frankly, I could use their insight." He raked a hand through his hair. "The one bit of good news is in an officer-related homicide, every possible law enforcement agency around will assist with the case. The bad news is we don't know who we're searching for. That's why I want Teddy and Derek in on this. They're very good at finding overlooked clues."

Her head swam. "Of course. Whatever you think is best. I just can't believe this has happened. Those men were innocent. They weren't part of this. Why did he have to kill them?"

JT placed his arm around her and drew her close. "He's unstable, Faith. To someone like that, killing means nothing. It doesn't matter that they had nothing to do with anything. They were standing in the way of his getting to you."

Faith leaned against him and closed her eyes. She could hear his steady heartbeat. Tonight she needed his strength more than ever.

"When I left Austin, I was so scared. I didn't know where to go. There was no one to turn to for help. I was terrified he'd come after me and kill me, so I got in my car and drove as far away as I could. I ended up in Billings, Montana. For a time, well, it seemed to work. I changed my name, settled in, found a job and started to think maybe I'd overreacted…."

When her voice trailed off, he gently stroked her hair. "Go on," he said.

"A short time later, he called again. After the second hang-up, well, I became suspicious of every stranger I met on the street. Since I couldn't remember his face, he could be anyone. Then I came home from work one day and found a candlelit dinner waiting for me, along with a note that said, *You belong to me.* I packed up everything and ran." She'd felt so alone. Having no one to turn to for help had been almost as bad as not knowing her stalker's identity.

"That must have been terrifying," JT said quietly.

It was. "I came close to giving up so many times. It was

one of the darkest points of my life, and then something remarkable happened. Right before I moved to Hope Island, I lived in Kansas for a time. One Sunday morning, I went for a drive in the country to clear my head and I spotted this little church outside of Benton, the town where I lived. I went in and sat in the back. JT, I can't explain it, but I just had a feeling of peace come over me, as I'd never experienced before. Everyone there was so nice. They welcomed me and didn't ask too many questions."

She sighed. "I went back the next week and the week after. It was the happiest I'd been since, well, since I can't remember. It changed my life. Because no matter how hopeless the situation seemed, I finally realized I didn't have to face it alone."

For a time, she'd actually begun to believe she might have a future there. She'd taken an online cooking class and discovered she loved it. At one point, she even thought about opening her own bakery. And then…

"Yet something did happen there. Otherwise you wouldn't have ended up on Hope Island. I take it he found you again."

That had been the worst experience since the attack. It scared her just thinking about it now. "Yes. He broke into my apartment one night and watched me while I slept. When I woke up and found him there, I froze. I didn't know what to do. I was certain he'd kill me and then he just left. The second I was sure he was gone, I grabbed everything and ran again."

She pulled away. "Every time he finds me the threats become more deadly. I'm afraid this time he's going to kill me." Her voice filled with panic.

JT tugged her back against his chest and she clung to him. "That's not happening because this time will be different. You have me…and round-the-clock protection."

She closed her eyes. She'd just rest here in the safety of his arms for a little while. She was so tired of fighting this battle.

SIX

He'd left the house phone's receiver in the kitchen. When it rang, he hurried to answer it before the noise woke Faith. She'd fallen asleep on the couch near him. She'd been emotionally drained.

He grabbed the phone and Will's cell number popped up on the caller ID.

"How are you two holding up?" Will asked, his voice holding traces of exhaustion.

JT glanced out the kitchen window. Dawn was just breaking. "Okay, I guess. Faith managed to sleep so that's something. Have you found out anything?"

Will blew out a sigh. "No. The rain washed away any DNA evidence there might have been. The officers didn't have time to defend themselves, JT. It was an ambush. I would have called earlier, but I had to notify their families. That was…difficult."

"I'm sorry. That had to be hard. I still can't believe it. I went to the academy with Samuels. He was a good man."

"They both were. This is a devastating blow to the department. At least the fire ended up contained to the downstairs area, thanks in part to the rain. The fire department got it out pretty quickly, and I do have a bit of good news for you. The blaze only destroyed the kitchen and part of the downstairs. Hopefully, Faith can salvage some of her things."

"I guess that's something," JT added quietly. However, in light of everything else, a few personal items didn't seem very important. He realized that he'd almost forgotten to mention a pertinent detail about the night of the fire. "I might have some good news for you, too. Faith told me she heard someone moving around downstairs right before I arrived. I'm hoping he left some footprints behind."

"I'll have my men check on it. Did she remember anything else?"

"She said she heard something like an explosion. I'm thinking he must have thrown a bottle filled with gasoline through the kitchen window. She remembered hearing the alarm go off, but only for a few minutes. Either the explosion took it out or the killer disarmed it."

"Makes sense. I'm thinking he killed my two men first to eliminate the threat, and then went after Faith." He drew in an audible breath. "I've been on the force for a lot of years and I've never seen a case quite like this."

JT had to agree. "The acts of violence are escalating. Whatever Faith has locked away in her memory has him acting like a cornered animal. He has nothing to lose. That's why I'm going to move Faith to a safe house as soon as I can make the arrangements."

"That's a good idea. He knows she's here on the island and he's determined enough to find her again." Will voiced JT's fears aloud.

"Exactly. I've asked Derek to do more digging into the details of the murders. He'll be stopping by to give me a status update in a few hours. Hopefully, we'll know more then."

"Good. We need answers fast. I have a call in to the Austin police. I should hear something from them soon."

JT said a silent prayer of thanks. "Good, because right now, nothing about this case makes sense."

"Right. The fire chief said he could probably clear the house this afternoon if everything goes well. Faith should be able to get some of her things then if the weather holds. I'm expecting the governor to issue a complete evacuation of the island anytime now."

JT ran a frustrated hand through his hair. "We knew it was coming, but it's still the last thing we need right now."

"Yes. Keep your eyes open. I hate to sound like the voice of doom and gloom, but I think the worst is still ahead of us."

After JT hung up, he checked on Faith. She hadn't moved since he'd left her. Ollie had positioned himself on top of her feet, but opened one eye and let out a halfhearted growl when JT covered Faith with a blanket.

"It's only me, boy. You're doing a good job."

Ollie settled down and began to snooze once more.

Catching a nap wasn't going to be an option for JT. Instead, he went back to the kitchen and made a pot of coffee. At a loss as to what to do next, he needed God's strength and guidance now more than ever.

He opened his Bible to the concordance, found the word *strength*, and looked up the Bible verse Isaiah 40:29–31, *God supplies power to the weak.*

Was there ever a soul as weak as he was tonight?

JT closed his eyes and prayed. *Lord, I need You. I'm not sure I can protect her on my own. Please help me.* He knew he'd lost his way spiritually. After Emily's death, he'd blamed God and himself for what had happened. He'd done his best to write God out of his life. Yet when troubles came into his life that were too much to bear, like the resurfacing of all his old insecurities, he found himself praying and asking for God's guidance. Each time he prayed a sense of calm settled over him. He'd experienced it before many times. God had a way of carrying those whose sorrows became overwhelming.

Faith didn't think sleep would be possible and yet somehow she'd fallen asleep on the couch. In spite of everything, knowing JT was close by gave her a feeling of peace.

She sat up and pushed the blanket away. The fire in the fireplace had died to embers, yet the room was still warm.

The smell of fresh-brewed coffee wafted in from the kitchen.

Ollie lay curled up on top of her feet. The second she moved, he hopped into her lap. Ollie was being overprotective of her. God blessed animals with the ability to sense when their human companions were hurting. Ollie had certainly figured it out.

She gathered the Pug in her arms. "Come on, boy. Let's go find JT."

When she walked into the kitchen, she stopped dead in her tracks. JT stood over by the window with his back to her, lost in thought and unaware of her. It struck her again just how handsome he was.

Ollie let out a little whimper and she let him go. JT turned slowly toward her. The seriousness of what he'd been pondering etched grooves around his mouth. She wanted to ask if he had bad news, but she was too afraid.

Their eyes met and held. Tension seeped into every pore of Faith's body. Old longings resurfaced. The ones she told herself she'd laid to rest.

He came over to where she stood and touched her cheek. She closed her eyes and breathed in the scent of him. He smelled like soap and outdoors—the ocean. Strength itself.

He was close enough for her to see when the need to comfort turned to something more. His hand lingered a second longer on her cheek and then cupped her face. After a moment's hesitation, he brought her close. He touched his lips to hers and stilled. Her eyes fluttered open and they watched each other for a moment. Then she was kissing him and he was kissing her. The world around them fell away. It took longer than it should have for her to realize he was the one to break off the kiss.

He cleared his throat. "I should probably say I'm sorry about that, but I'm not. I don't regret kissing you, Faith. I hope you don't, either."

She loved his honesty. She met his gaze unflinchingly. "I don't regret it."

He let go of the breath he had been holding, waiting for her answer. "Good. Coffee's fresh. Want some?"

She couldn't quite match his nonchalance. Being near him reminded her of things she'd given up on for her own life. Things like companionship. Love. Someone to be there for you when you needed him.

"Oh, yes."

He chuckled at the slight edge of desperation in her tone. "If you're hungry I could make us some breakfast."

"No, coffee's fine."

He pointed to the kitchen table. "Sit. I'll get it for you."

She sank down in the nearest chair and reality intruded into her thoughts. What if JT were wrong and they weren't able to discover the identity of the person trying to kill her? What if she had to run again? She didn't think she could bear to leave again.

Faith glanced out the kitchen window to the ocean beyond. Today the ocean was gray and angry. Clouds hung low in the sky.

JT handed her a cup and she took it with visibly unsteady fingers.

He pulled another chair out across from her. "Look at

me." After a long moment, she did as he asked. "This *will* end. I give you my promise. You just have to do your part. You can't give up."

He was sacrificing so much to help her. She owed him her life. She'd fight until there was no more fight left in her. "Okay," she said at last.

"Good. I've asked my business partners to stop by this morning. I've brought them up to speed on everything. I'm hoping between the four of us, we can start to fit some pieces together."

He'd no sooner gotten the words out than the doorbell rang. "And that'll be them now. I'll be right back." He left her to answer the door.

Faith's thoughts sped at a mile a minute. So much had happened and yet everything from the night before seemed like a blur.

JT came back with two men. "Teddy, Derek, this is Faith McKenzie. Faith, this is Teddy Warren and Derek Thomas. Without these two men, there wouldn't be a Wyatt Securities. They've been with me since the beginning."

Teddy Warren stuck out his hand. He had to be close to JT's age and prematurely graying. Everything about the man screamed someone who possessed a bundle of energy and struggled to control it.

"It's good to meet you, Faith. I'm sorry it has to be under these circumstances."

"Thank you. Me, too."

The second man, Derek Thomas, was average in both height and build and as different from Teddy Warren as possible. There was a quietness about the dark-haired man that hinted at someone who rarely spoke unless he had something worth saying.

"Faith, if you're ready, we have a few questions for you,"

JT said. "Let's go to my office. There's less clutter in there and we'll have more room."

JT closed the door, cleared a stack of papers from the last remaining chair and sat down. "Did you find out anything about the medication?" he asked Derek curiously.

"I did and I have some strange news for you."

A sliver of trepidation slipped into the pit of JT's stomach. "What is it?"

"Turns out Zyban has nothing to do with helping memory return. Just the opposite, in fact. It's an antismoking drug."

Faith shot JT a startled look. "I can't believe it. It doesn't make any sense."

JT had suspected something was off about the drug, but nothing prepared him for this. "What would be the benefit of prescribing such a drug?"

"I don't think there are any," Derek told them. "I checked with two different doctors and they both confirmed it. And get this—one of the known side effects for Zyban is short-term memory loss."

Faith's eyes widened in disbelief. "I don't understand why my doctor would prescribe such a medicine."

JT turned to her. "What did the doctor tell you about the medication?"

She shook her head. "That's just it…I never actually spoke to the doctor about it. When I got home from the hospital, the pills were in my bag with Dr. Stephens's name on the prescription. There were instructions on how often to take the pills, along with how to refill them online. With everything that happened, I guess I never really questioned why no one spoke to me about taking the drug."

"If it wasn't prescribed, then how'd it end up in your bag with the doctor's name on it?" Derek wondered aloud.

"I mean, in order for you to keep getting the prescription filled, a doctor would have to sign off on it."

"Yes, I guess so."

JT had an idea. "Do we have your consent to get your medical records sent over?" he asked her.

She didn't hesitate. "Of course."

"Good. Once we have the records, I'm willing to believe there won't be any prescription mentioned in them. I'm going to try to speak with the doctor who treated you. His name may be on the prescription, but I don't think he prescribed the medicine."

Alarm showed in her eyes. "You think…*he* did this?"

"Exactly," JT said. "Whoever is stalking you is connected to the hospital in some way. How else would he be able to get those drugs to you in the first place and keep the prescription going? We just have to figure out what the connection is."

"It certainly makes sense," Derek agreed. "I'd say whoever rigged the prescription is banking on your not regaining any of your memories of the attack."

JT wondered what was going to happen when the killer learned Faith had stopped taking the meds. If he hadn't already…

"Will's got his hands full right now. It may be a few days before he can get any details on the case from the detectives who investigated the murders. Teddy, can you dig around a little?"

"I'm already on it. So far, I've run into a wall," he told them. "A blue wall, to be exact. I have a friend who's a former Austin detective and he remembers the Jennings case, just not too many of the details. I'll keep trying."

"Good. If you have to push a little harder, do it."

Teddy glanced at his watch and grimaced. "I need to get going. I'm taking Brenda and the baby over to Derek's place in Alfred until the storm passes. They should be safe there."

"I'll go with you," Derek said. "I need to clean the place up a bit, otherwise Brenda won't be able to sleep. I'll start poking into the Jennings' past and see what I can come up with."

"That'd be great." JT rose and followed his partners to the door. "I'll be right back, okay?" he told Faith.

She nodded. "Thank you both for everything you're doing to help me." She looked exhausted beyond belief. She probably hadn't gotten a good night's rest in years.

"Hang in there." Derek tried to reassure her.

Her smile didn't seem genuine. "I'll do my best."

JT waited until they reached the front door. "I didn't want to say this in front of Faith, but we don't have much time. We need answers fast before this person strikes again and the weather seems to be playing a big factor in all of this. Be careful, you two. We don't even know who we're dealing with. It could be anyone and I don't want anything to happen to either of you."

Teddy patted his shoulder. "Don't worry about us. You focus on keeping Faith and yourself safe. You are the closest person to her right now. In my book, that puts you right in the killer's sights."

JT closed the door and went back to his office. Faith hadn't moved since they'd left. She stared into space with the weight of the world on her shoulders.

He sat down next to her. "I know this is hard."

She stared at her clasped hands. "JT, I'm so scared. I—I just want this to end." She was crying and he'd give anything to take her pain away.

JT brushed a calloused thumb over her cheek. "I know you do. I'm sure right now, it's impossible to imagine it ever ending, but it will."

"And how many more innocent people will have to die before that happens?" she said wearily and covered her eyes with her hand. "This is so unfair. Those two officers' deaths weren't fair. Rachel's and Carl's weren't. None of this is fair."

"I know it isn't."

A storm of emotions—fear, uncertainty, acceptance—warred for control. After what felt like an eternity, she gave him a faint smile and his pulse beat a little faster at the sight of it.

"Thank you," she whispered.

"You're very welcome." He knew he'd do whatever it took, everything within his power to keep her safe.

SEVEN

Once the fire department finished inspecting the house, JT drove Faith over to pick up some of her things. When they pulled into Faith's driveway, Will was there waiting for them. The clouds from earlier had dissipated. A gorgeous blue sky and calm seas made it impossible to believe anything bad could be headed their way.

Will's people had cleared away the patrol car. With the exception of the charred downstairs, there was no sign of the terror that had taken place in her home less than twenty-four hours earlier.

They got out of the SUV and went over to Will. "Any news yet?" JT asked as he glanced up at the house.

Will shook his head. "No. We had a forensics team go over the truck inside and out. There was nothing. I'm sure he wore gloves. We did find a footprint in the kitchen that didn't belong to any of our people and you said you didn't go near the kitchen." He paused briefly. "CSI took a photograph of it and our technician was able to confirm with some certainty it's a man's size-10 Rockwood work boot. Pretty commonplace around here."

"What about the ballistics report?"

Will didn't answer right away. Both JT and Faith stared at him. Something was wrong.

"What is it?" JT asked.

"He used an AK-47 M4 assault rifle. The shell casings matched the ones he fired at you."

Faith had no idea what the significance of the model was, but she could see it meant something to JT.

"It's one of the standard weapons used by most SWAT teams," he told her.

"Do you think he's a cop?" That would certainly explain how there'd been no evidence left behind. No suspects in the Austin murders. It made sense. A cop would be able to track her down easily enough.

JT shook his head. "Let's not jump to conclusions. That type of weapon isn't exclusive to law enforcement."

"But still, it's a possibility. Wouldn't you have to register a weapon like that?"

Will shrugged. "Yes, unless it was purchased illegally. I'm checking records now. Hopefully something will come of it."

Once again, the killer seemed one step ahead of them.

Will headed for the front of the house. "Let's go in this way. I'm not sure the back is structurally stable."

The second Faith stepped into the foyer, the horror of that night surged back. She'd come close to dying. So had JT. He'd risked his life to save her. What about the next time?

JT touched her arm. "Don't go there. We're both safe."

She smiled at his attempt to reassure her. "Yes. Thankfully."

Behind them, Will cleared his throat. "We notified the realtor handling the house. She's still not sure what they're going to do with the place. Most of the stuff in the kitchen and in the back of the house is ruined. The fire never reached upstairs, though. I can't guarantee you'll be able to use any of your clothes ever again with all the smoke, but there might be some mementos worth saving. I need to check out a few things down here. You two go ahead."

Faith followed JT upstairs while the chief stayed below.

A heavy scent of smoke clung to everything. The smoke had tinted her bedroom's cream-colored walls gray. She looked around in dismay. She didn't know where to start.

JT came up behind her. "Hey, it's just stuff. You and Ollie are fine. You can replace everything else."

That much was certainly true. She went over to the table next to her bed to get her watch. JT's cell phone was there as well. She handed it to him. "Hopefully it's not ruined."

"It'll be fine. This one's supposed to be virtually inde-structible." He shoved it in his pocket while she glanced around the room and noticed something missing from the top of her dresser.

JT had seen her hesitation. "What's wrong?"

She went over to the dresser. "There used to be a small picture frame here. It's missing."

"What was in it?"

"A photo of me and Rachel taken right before…that night. I'm almost certain it was here when we left last night. Why would he take it? When did he take it?" Was he hoping to keep some trophy from that horrible night? The thought of it made her sick.

"I don't know. I'll tell Will about it. Let's get your stuff. We shouldn't stay here much longer."

She gathered a few personal items and some toiletries and tossed them into a bag. The picture of herself with Rachel was the only thing of any emotional value.

JT took the bag from her. "Ready?"

She glanced around the room that had been her home for just a short time. Once again, she was running. "Yes."

They went downstairs together and found Will waiting for them in the foyer.

"Has anyone been in the house since the firefighters cleared it?" JT asked.

The question surprised the other man. "No. The fire department had their people out here all night watching to make sure the fire didn't restart. Why?"

"Someone took a picture from Faith's dresser. It was a photo of Faith with Rachel Jennings."

"I don't think anyone from the fire department would have a reason to take it, but I'll talk to the fire chief to see if he knows anything. Does the picture have any special meaning to you?"

As hard as she tried, she couldn't remember details of her friendship with Rachel. "I don't know. I kept it because it was the only thing I had of the two of us together."

Will walked with them back to the SUV. "Depending on what type of direct hit the other islands take, the hurricane could either blow itself out or turn back out to sea and continue to grow stronger. Either way, this is the last place Faith needs to be when the power goes out."

JT nodded in agreement as he held the door open for her. "I've called my friend Mark. He has a house outside of Whaler's Point. He's out of the country for another month and he told me to use the place for as long as we need. We'll leave in the morning." With everything that was going on, remaining positive took every ounce of Faith's energy.

"At least Whaler's Point isn't in the storm's direct path as of yet. That's something," Will pointed out. "But you two still need to be careful. I don't know what to make of this predator, and without having a clear picture of what he looks like, we don't know where he might turn up next."

Faith felt JT stealing glances her way as they drove through town. She knew she'd been unusually quiet since they'd left her house, and it was due in large part to their earlier kiss. It had left her feeling a little off balance... and she just couldn't get that unforgettable encounter out of her head. She wondered if JT had felt the same rush of attraction for her that she had for him. It made her wish for what couldn't be. So many things stood in their way, and the biggest obstacle of all was her uncertainty about whether she had taken part in the Jennings' murders. With so much unsettled, it would be a big mistake to give in to the desires of her heart.

"Are you okay?" The gravelly sound of his voice pulled her out of her troubled thoughts. She slowly nodded, yet she couldn't quite make eye contact. She didn't want him to see the struggle going on inside her.

When they passed the cutoff to his house, Faith shifted in her seat uneasily. "Where are we going?"

He looked her way. "Since most of your clothes were ruined, I thought we could stop by the clothing store downtown and pick up a few things."

The thought of shopping for clothes with JT felt a little too personal, yet she knew he was only trying to help. She leaned back in her seat and watched the light traffic pass by as she tried to calm her crazy heartbeat.

It was off-season for tourists so the town was definitely experiencing a down period. With the impending hurricane, she had a feeling things were about to get worse.

JT parked the Suburban in front of Island Dreams, got out of the car and opened her door. "It's not much, but I'm sure you can find something that works."

When his fingers brushed her arm, she moved away. She was acting like a schoolgirl who had just had her first kiss and yet she couldn't seem to help it. Everything about her reaction to JT scared her.

He seemed to sense it as well. "I'll wait for you over

by the window. I want to keep an eye on what's going on outside." He stepped away and she could breathe normally again.

Faith went over to the sale rack and began browsing through the items while JT checked messages on his phone. She'd worked at a clothing store in Benton before the move to Hope Island. The owner had taken Faith under her wing and let her stay at the apartment above the store rent-free. In exchange, Faith opened the store each morning for her. Because of the woman's generosity, she had managed to save a nice nest egg, which allowed her to take her time finding a job when she moved to the island. She'd gotten used to dressing in jeans and T-shirts.

Faith picked out several pairs of jeans and half a dozen pastel T-shirts, along with other necessary items, then paid for them.

"Did you find everything you needed?" JT asked politely as he took the bag from her.

She followed him outside and back to the Suburban. "Yes, thank you. I'm all set."

"Good." He unlocked the door, put the bag inside and closed it again.

Finally, she glanced at him. The look in his blue eyes sent her heart racing. "What are you doing?"

"Relax." He leaned against the Suburban and tugged her closer. "We could have some rough days ahead of us, so I thought maybe we could just take a walk along the beach and unwind." He brushed a strand of her hair away from her face. "What do you think? Want to take a stroll with me?"

In JT Wyatt, she found what she'd always been searching for, and it scared her to death. She wanted to spend this time with him. Only him. She swallowed hard and took the hand he offered her. "I'd love to."

"Good, because there's this great stretch of beach a couple of blocks from here. It's been used as a backdrop in several movies. It's a shame to live on Hope Island and not see it." She could feel color creeping into her cheeks and she looked away.

He laughed huskily. "You are awfully pretty when you're blushing, Faith McKenzie."

When they reached the beach, she stopped and took in the stunning view. The soft sand spread out before her, but it was the pristine blue water beyond that was the most amazing.

She realized JT was watching her reaction. "It's beautiful. I can't believe it. It's so different from our beach and yet we're not that far away."

"I know. There are a few beaches scattered around Maine that come close, but none of them are as picturesque as this one. People come from all over the world to see this stretch of shoreline."

She could certainly understand that. "It makes me want to take my shoes off and feel the sand between my toes." She snatched a quick glance at JT and laughed. "Is that silly or what?"

He chuckled as well. "It's not silly at all. In fact, I'll race you."

"I beg your pardon?" At first, she thought he was joking until he grabbed one foot and pulled off his shoe. She watched in disbelief for a second and then they were racing to see who could get their shoes off first.

By the time they were both barefoot, they were laughing so hard it was difficult to catch their breath.

JT grabbed her hand and held it. "Come on. Let's get our feet wet."

She nodded and they walked down to the water's edge. Faith waited while JT stuck his foot in and cringed.

She giggled at his expression. "Is it cold?"

"Freezing," he said and splashed some water on her foot.

"JT." She squeaked and jumped backwards several steps, but he caught her before she got away.

He tugged her close and wrapped his arms around her. Suddenly both of them weren't laughing anymore.

"JT." She exhaled his name right before he lowered his head and kissed her and she forgot about everything but the man standing close to her.

This is wrong, her head told her, but her heart just wanted to stay here with him for a little while longer. She wanted to feel normal. Special. He made her feel both those things and so much more.

JT lifted his head and gazed into her eyes. "We should probably get going." But he didn't move. "We need to pack and get ready for the trip tomorrow and I don't trust being here in the open like this too long."

"Yes." She sounded breathless, as if she'd been running a marathon.

He cupped her face and leaned in to kiss the tip of her nose and she sighed softly. Just for a little while, she'd felt happy and carefree again. He turned to leave but she reached up and touched his cheek. "No, wait."

His eyes searched hers, filled with concern. "What is it?"

"Nothing. I just wanted to thank you. I know this has been hard for you, too. You've risked your life for me." She pointed toward the ocean. "You didn't have to do this, but I'm so glad you did."

JT pulled the SUV behind the house and glanced around at the surrounding area cloaked in darkness. Everything appeared as they'd left it, yet he couldn't shake the feeling someone might be watching them.

Faith noticed his uneasiness. "What's wrong?"

"I'm not sure. Maybe nothing. Let's just go inside." He got out of the SUV and went around to her side. He took another quick look around, but nothing was out of place. Was he just being paranoid?

After they were inside and he secured both door locks, the niggling feeling didn't go away. "I'm just going to check things outside to be on the safe side."

Faith's eyes widened in alarm. "Do you think someone is following us?"

He did his best to reassure her. "No, there's no one following us. I just want to make sure everything's okay."

She grabbed his arm in a death grip. "JT, don't go out there by yourself. Let me come with you."

JT tried not to show his concern. "You can't, Faith. I need you to wait here. Why don't you put on some coffee and when I get back we'll talk."

After a second, she gave in. "Okay."

The churning ball in the pit of his stomach assured him he wasn't overreacting.

JT followed Faith to the kitchen and closed all the shades. "I'll be right back. Make sure you lock up behind me."

Once outside, JT took his time, combing every square inch of the property around the house, searching for footprints or any indication someone had tried to break into the house. There was nothing.

He went to the SUV to retrieve the bag he kept in the back. It held some tools of the trade. He dug out his binoculars and panned the wooded space in front of the house. There was no sign of movement. The sooner they were on the road and off the island, the better he'd feel. Hopefully, they could be on their way to Mark's place as soon as dawn broke.

He knocked once on the back door. "It's me, Faith."

She quickly unlocked it. "Is everything all right?"

"Yes, I think so." Ollie came into the kitchen and watched them before digging into his kibble. If Ollie wasn't worried, why was he?

Pull it together, Wyatt.

JT glanced up and caught Faith watching him. She knew he was hiding something, which meant he was definitely losing his touch. He smiled and decided to change the subject onto safer ground. "I'll take that coffee now."

She grabbed a couple of cups from the cabinet and poured the coffee and they sat at the table together.

As he sipped his coffee, he couldn't shake his uneasiness.

"I've been thinking we shouldn't wait until morning to leave. The faster we get on the road the better chance we have at beating the traffic leaving the island before the storm. I'll just shower and pack some things and we can be on our way."

She set down her cup. "JT, what aren't you telling me? Did you see something out there?"

He decided to tell her the truth. "That's just it. There's no sign of anyone trying to get in. As far as I could tell, no one followed us from town, but my gut tells me we need to keep moving. Are you up for starting the trip tonight?"

She studied his expression for a long moment before agreeing. She trusted him completely and that freaked him out. "Yes. That's a good idea, and I could use a shower, too. I smell like smoke. I'll be right back." She scooped up her purchases from where she'd dropped them and headed for the guest bathroom upstairs with Ollie at her heels.

JT flipped off the coffeemaker, grabbed his overnight bag from the downstairs closet and went up to his room. In the bathroom attached to his room, he took a quick shower then threw a handful of things he'd need for the trip into the bag. He took the Glock from his dresser where he'd laid it and stuffed it inside his jacket pocket. Then he carried the bag downstairs and dropped it by his office door.

He'd need his laptop for work and as a means of communication in case cell service was disrupted. He unplugged the computer and opened his desk drawer to grab a thumb drive. The photo of his wife was the first thing he saw. He'd placed it there shortly after Emily's death when he couldn't bear to see it every day and remember what he'd lost. He picked up the photo and touched Emily's blond hair. "I love you, babe. I'll always love you, but I think it's time I moved on with my life. I've been stuck in the past until now. Blaming myself for what happened. I know you wouldn't want that."

Emily's smiling face looked back at him. It was as if she were telling him it was okay to let go.

Faith noticed the light on in JT's office. She stuck her head in the door and saw him standing next to his desk holding a photo. She stopped dead in her tracks. Something in his expression made it seem like a personal moment. She turned to leave when he glanced up. Their eyes met. The hurt in his eyes tore at her heart. "I'm sorry. I didn't mean to intrude."

"No, it's all right. Come in."

She went over to where he stood. He held a photo of a woman. She smiled at the person behind the camera, her silver-blond hair blowing in the breeze. She was dressed in a sage-green sweater, which matched her eyes perfectly. In the background were trees colored in an array of reds and golds.

"Is that Emily?" Faith asked.

"Yes." There was a catch in his voice.

"She's beautiful, JT."

He nodded. "She was beautiful. Inside and out. You'd never guess she was a cop, but she could hold her own against any criminal around, and yet Emily had a gentle presence about her that I always found comforting. It didn't matter how crazy our jobs got, I could count on her to be a calming influence." He exhaled sharply. "In her spare time, she worked with battered women and runaway kids. She had the biggest heart. She was always willing to help someone, whether it was a troubled child or a stray cat."

Faith couldn't begin to imagine the depth of his grief. She touched his face gently and he leaned in to her touch.

"What happened to her?" She regretted the question when she saw the pain flit across his face again.

"I'm sorry. I shouldn't have asked." She held her breath. JT had told her Emily was murdered, but the details of it must be something horrible. It had left an indelible brand of sadness in his eyes.

"No, it's okay. It doesn't hurt so much anymore. Emily and I practically grew up on Hope Island. When we were kids it was always Emily, Liz and me hanging out together. Emily and I became high school sweethearts and got married right after graduation," he said with a brittle smile.

JT focused on the photo for the moment, completely lost in the past and unaware of her.

"One night we were on our way home from work. We needed something—I think it was something ridiculous like milk. I stopped at the corner store. It was raining. Neither one of us wanted to get out. We did rock, paper, scissors to decide who had to go out in the rain, mostly because Emily refused to let me do the 'manly thing,' as she called it. I won. She lost." A muscle worked in his cheek and his voice dropped to a ragged whisper. "Emily walked into the store and right into a holdup. It was just a couple of kids. They freaked. Took the clerk hostage. Emily drew her weapon. It all happened so fast…I didn't even know what was going on until I heard the shots. By the time I reached her side, it was too late. I held my wife and watched her die."

Unexpected tears filled her eyes. It was easy to see he blamed himself for his wife's death. "Oh, JT, I'm so sorry. But it wasn't your fault. It could just as easily have been you who died. It was just a terrible tragedy."

His smile didn't quite reach his eyes. "I know. At least in my head I do, but for a long time I couldn't accept it. I blamed God. Myself. Everyone except for the people responsible for Emily's death. I almost lost it." He raked a hand through his hair. "I know how destructive blame can be, and if it weren't for my family and friends, well, I'm not so sure where I'd be today."

"I'm sure they were a salvation," she said softly.

"Absolutely. They stood beside me during my darkest hours, and on top of that, my sister kept me in church when I wanted to write it off along with God. Liz wouldn't let me do either of those things. I'm glad she didn't."

She squeezed his hand. "Me, too." She glanced at the photo again. "I wish I'd known Emily. She sounds like a wonderful person."

"She was and a good judge of character. She would have admired your strength."

Strength was the last thing Faith associated with herself.

"You're very strong. You may not realize it, but you have more strength than many people I know. It's one of the first things that drew me to you, along with your overwhelming desire to survive. Faced with what you've been through, most people would have given up long ago. You didn't. You have no idea how special you are, Faith."

She wrapped her arms around his waist and held him close. She wanted to be the woman he believed she was.

She closed her eyes and listened to the steady beat of his heart against her ear. "I'm so glad I met you, JT. You have no idea how long I've prayed God would send someone like you into my life. You're God's answer. He sent me you. *You're* His gift." She raised her head. There were tears in her eyes but she didn't care if he saw them. She wanted him to know how important he was to her.

He face twisted in pain. "No one's ever called me a gift before, but you've got it wrong. I've been floundering for a while, since Emily's death. Tonight, I realized I never really made peace with her passing. I just buried it deep in my heart and threw myself into my work. I figured if I could save enough people then maybe I could make up for losing Emily."

She of all people understood the power of guilt. "Your wife would be so proud of you. You help people who can't help themselves. You're giving me back my life. Until now...*you*...well, I thought I would spend the rest of my life running away from someone I couldn't remember. I don't think I can ever thank you enough for what you've done."

She caught her breath at the smoldering attraction she saw in his eyes. JT hesitated a moment longer then leaned in and touched his lips to hers. Her eyes closed. The embrace was sweet and tender—JT was obviously holding back—but his kiss held so many promises she couldn't let herself believe in just yet.

They each had secrets in their lives. He'd shared his. She couldn't do the same, because the biggest secret of all remained locked away in her lost memories. With all her heart, she hoped she wouldn't learn the monster they'd been chasing all along was the one peering back at her in the mirror each day.

EIGHT

"I'm going to make sure everything's turned off before we leave. Why don't you fix some sandwiches for the road? I'll be right back." JT hated letting her go, yet ever since they had gotten back to the house, he couldn't escape his uneasiness. It had been his constant companion.

While Faith made sandwiches, he checked the rooms upstairs first. Nothing appeared out of place. Maybe it was just the numerous unanswered questions revolving around the case that were getting to him. No matter what the reason, he needed to get a grip. He couldn't afford to keep second-guessing himself.

Halfway down the stairs he heard it. A noise coming from outside. It sounded like footsteps on the front porch.

JT covered the remaining steps as quietly as he could. He found Faith in the kitchen and put his finger to his lips before she could speak.

He came close and whispered against her ear. "I think someone's outside. I'm going to check it out. Call Will. Tell him we need help right away. Try to keep Ollie quiet."

JT moved away but she grabbed his arm. "No, JT, you can't go out there. That's what he wants. He'll kill you. Please, wait for backup."

"I'll be fine. Hurry, Faith. There's not much time."

JT drew his weapon and slipped out the back door as stealthily as possible. He took a second to absorb his surroundings. With the recent rain, a thick white fog had descended on the beach and an eerie silence enveloped him.

He barely cleared the bottom step when out of the corner of his eye he detected movement. Before he had time to react, something hard smashed against his arm—the one holding the Glock. Pain shot up the arm like a lightning bolt. The gun flew from his hand and out of sight.

JT staggered backwards but kept from losing his balance. His injured arm hung at his side; even the slightest movement hurt like crazy. It wasn't broken but he couldn't be sure how bad the damage was.

His heartbeat echoed in his ears as he searched the darkness for his attacker. It was next to impossible to see more than a handful of feet in any direction and the fog distorted every sound. Then he heard a footstep.

JT whipped around just as the figure of a man dressed entirely in dark clothing with a ski mask covering his face emerged from the fog next to him. The man held something in his hand. When he raised it, JT caught the glint of a knife's blade in the light from the kitchen.

The man charged toward him. JT scarcely had time to brace himself as the assailant's body slammed against his injured arm. JT shrieked in pain and his knees buckled beneath him. He dropped to the ground, the impact of the blow driving air from his body.

Before JT had time to get to his feet, the man was on top of him, the weapon poised above his head. JT grabbed the arm holding the knife. His attacker seemed to possess superhuman strength, like someone high on drugs. JT felt himself losing the advantage. The knife inched closer to his chest. The man leaned in and JT could see the rage in his eyes.

JT realized if he wanted to live, he'd have to use his damaged arm.

Lord, please give me strength.

He gritted his teeth as burning pain ripped up his arm and beads of sweat broke out on his forehead. JT braced his injured arm against the man's shoulder, and pushed with all his strength. The pain was excruciating but the guy fell backwards. JT scrambled after him, his breath labored. The man recovered his balance just as quickly and jumped to his knees. He let out a low growl like a cornered animal.

JT dove for the knife, but the man pulled it back. JT fell forward and flipped over on his back before the assailant pounced on him once more, wielding the knife wildly, and further confirming JT's belief the man was either high on drugs or mentally unstable. JT dodged to his left before the knife could strike him dead-on, but he wasn't quick enough to miss the blade entirely. It slashed across his right side.

It felt as if a razor blade had sliced through his body. Immediately, blood oozed from the wound. Although he had no idea how deep the gash was, JT sucked in a breath and shoved the man's chest with all his strength. The assailant fell away and JT scrambled across the ground, putting space between them.

In the distance, JT heard sirens blaring. *Thank You, God.*

The man seemed oblivious to the noise and determined to finish JT off. He let out another low growl and charged JT again, hitting him with the full brunt of his weight. JT fell backwards into the sand and the assailant landed on JT's injured side.

JT grabbed the man's arm—the one holding the knife—and the knife slipped a little, but that didn't seem to slow him down any.

He shoved the knife closer to JT's face. It was inches away. JT wouldn't be able to fight him off much longer.

"What do you want? Why are you stalking her?" JT managed to get the words out. The man stopped and stared right at him. As the sirens drew closer, the attacker finally became aware of them. He jumped to his feet and tossed the knife toward the water, then he took off running in the opposite direction from the squad cars descending on the house.

JT staggered to his feet. He'd survived the ambush, but one thing was apparent. This man was extremely danger-ous and he had nothing to lose. JT touched his injured side as proof and blood covered his hand. He found the Glock where it had landed and kept his eyes focused on the door, leaning heavily against the railing. Each step drained his remaining strength. Blood trickled from the wound. Two more steps. Just two more steps.

Sirens sounded along the coastal road, shattering the eerie silence surrounding the house.

"Faith, open the door. It's me."

The moment she heard JT's voice she ran to the door and yanked it open. JT all but fell into her arms. "What happened?" When she flipped on the light, blood covered most of the right side of his shirt. She clamped a hand over her mouth. "JT, you're hurt!"

The Glock fell from his hand to the floor. "It looks worse than it is. He had a knife. He came out of nowhere. Caught me off guard. He hit me with something—maybe a piece of driftwood." His voice sounded faint and she no-ticed his right arm hung close to his body.

"You need to sit down." Faith half dragged, half carried JT over to the kitchen table. His face was distorted in pain as he lowered his tall frame into the chair.

He could have killed JT. The killer might still be out there somewhere watching for his next opportunity.

Faith carefully removed JT's jacket. The knife had shredded the right side of his shirt.

JT turned white as a sheet and sweat beaded along his forehead.

"We need to get you to a hospital right away."

"No, it's not bad. Just a flesh wound."

She wasn't nearly as convinced. The wound appeared serious. JT fumbled with the buttons on his shirt then gave up.

"Here, let me do it." She undid the buttons and gently pulled off the shirt. An ugly, three-inch-long gash ran down his side. "JT, you need stitches."

"There's no time. We need to get off the island as soon as possible. There will be EMTs dispatched to the call. I'll have one of them examine it."

Before he finished speaking, four armed officers burst through the door, followed by Will. The officers lowered their weapons when they spotted JT.

"Get Ed in here right away," Will ordered when he got a good look at his friend. He came and knelt in front of JT. "How bad is it?"

JT's jaw clenched in pain. "Not bad, just a surface wound, I think. It just needs to be cleaned and bandaged." JT tried to sit up, winced and fell back in his seat. "And maybe something for the pain."

The EMT dropped his gear next to JT and began examining the wound. "It's right on the border of needing stitches. We should probably get you to the hospital. The good news is, your arm isn't broken, just severely bruised. It's going to hurt like crazy for a few days, though. I can give you a sling to help keep it immobile."

"No hospital, Ed. There's no time. We have to get on the road.

Ed glanced up at Will. "I don't recommend traveling in your condition."

JT shook his head. "It's not an option."

"Okay," Ed said at last. "I'll do what I can to close the wound. You'll need to keep a careful eye on it. If it gets any worse in the next twenty-four hours, you'll need to go to the hospital right away."

"Thanks, Ed," JT said in a strained voice.

"What happened out there?" Will asked.

"He came out of nowhere. He took me by surprise and smashed something against my arm. That's how I got this." JT jerked his head toward his bum arm. "When he charged at me, I realized he had a knife. We struggled and he got in a good lick, but I think the knife may have slipped in his hand. He could be injured, Will."

He gritted his teeth as Ed applied antiseptic to the wound. "And there is something else. He tossed the knife toward the ocean. I don't think it hit the water. Maybe he left some DNA behind."

Will motioned to the officer by the door. "Get some men to search the area by the water for the knife." The man nodded, then left to obey the order.

"Did you see his face?" Will asked.

JT shook his head. "No, he wore a mask that covered his face, and with the fog, well, it was hard to see much. I'd say he was about six-two to six-four and stocky build. Not much to go on, I know."

"That's different from the description Faith gave us. Are you sure, JT?"

JT's gaze collided with Faith and he nodded. "I'm positive. It stands to reason Faith's memory of that occasion might be a little fuzzy. It's been two years and she was scared to death."

Both men looked at her expectantly. She'd been so certain before. Had she been wrong? "I'm not sure. I'm sorry." She bit her lip. She couldn't believe how close to death JT had come once more. "Do you think he followed us here?"

JT sucked in breath as the EMT finished bandaging the wound. "It makes sense. He may have been watching us when we left your house. He could have tracked us here easily enough."

Someone from the forensics team came in, followed by the officer stationed by the door.

"We have the knife." The forensics team member held up a bloody knife in an evidence bag. "There's something else I think you should see, Chief Kelly."

Will headed after the officer and JT struggled to his feet.

"Where do you think you're going?" Will demanded.

"With you, of course."

The chief of police shook his head but didn't argue.

"JT…" Faith could see he was ready to collapse. Pain deepened the grooves around his mouth, even though he was trying not to show how badly it hurt.

He turned back and tried to appear strong for her. "Don't worry. I'm okay, and I'll be right back."

JT followed the men outside to his SUV. The forensics officer took out his flashlight and positioned the light on the hood of the vehicle. The man who attacked him had placed a bloody handprint right in the center of the hood.

"I think he may have made his first mistake. Let's hope he's in the system because we really need a break," Will said with a hint of excitement in his voice.

JT couldn't share his friend's enthusiasm. The handprint seemed staged to him. As if the man had deliberately placed it there. He doubted if they'd find a match for the prints. He glanced up at the sky above, filled with millions of glittering stars. The calm before the storm. He wished he could capture just a piece of the tranquility surrounding them now.

"You'd never guess a category 3 is expected to strike Hatton at any moment."

JT glanced over at Will in surprise. "Unbelievable. Things have been so crazy I haven't even listened to the weather. When did they upgrade it? Did everyone get off Hatton okay?"

"A couple of hours ago, and, yes, from the reports I'm hearing everyone is safely off the island so that's something. The governor issued the order of evacuation for Hope Island starting in the morning. I told Cynthia to take the kids tonight and go to her mother's in New York for a few days."

"Good thinking. I'm sure it'll be a relief for you to know they'll be safe."

"Yup, one less thing to worry about." Will rubbed a hand across his jaw.

JT held his injured side. Even though Ed had wrapped the wound tight, it still hurt like crazy.

"Are you sure you're going to be up to leaving tonight? You were hurt pretty bad in spite of what you want Faith to believe."

JT shook his head. "I don't think we have a choice. I need to get her off the island and away from this creep as soon as possible."

Will fished in his pocket and handed JT a set of keys. "Here, use my truck. I came straight from my house when Faith called. I'll get a ride to the precinct with one of my officers. It'll be hours before the CSI team is done processing your vehicle. You need to get on the road."

His friend's generosity humbled him at times. "Thanks, Will."

"I'll have my officers stay with you until you're ready to leave, then we'll escort you off the island. I've arranged to have two patrol cars stationed outside of Mark's place as long as I can. The chief of police at Whaler's Point is an old friend. Since we don't know for sure how he's keeping track of her, I spoke to these men personally and advised them not to tell anyone, not even their families, what they were doing. There's no way he'll find her through them, but keep your eyes open anyway. We haven't heard the last of this guy."

"Got it. And thanks, Will. We couldn't do any of this without you."

JT went back inside and found Faith anxiously pacing around his kitchen. When she spotted him, she stopped. "Anything?"

He came over to where she stood. "Will's team found a handprint on the SUV, and he thinks it could lead to the break we've been looking for, but we don't have anything concrete yet." He glanced at his watch. "If you're ready, we should be on our way. It's a long drive."

She didn't move. "You're hurt. Let me drive for a while. At least until you've had a chance to rest."

JT nodded slowly. "That's a good idea. Once we're on the road and I've rested, I'll be fine."

"You're not fine, JT. You almost died…" Her voice cracked with emotion.

JT gathered her close, his chin resting against her head. "I know you're feeling overwhelmed right now, but I'm okay. You've made the right choice, Faith. The only way to end this is to stand up and fight him with everything you have inside you."

More than anything, he wanted to protect her from what lay ahead. Instead, all he could do was help her find the courage to get through each difficult day as they came.

"I'm not sure I can fight anymore," she whispered against his chest.

"You can, because if you don't, you'll be running for the rest of your life. You're not a quitter, Faith. You can do this."

She pulled away and looked into his eyes. Something from his past, a long-forgotten feeling, closed in around him, making it impossible to draw air into his lungs.

She saw it, too. "What is it?"

He exhaled slowly and pulled her back against him. As much as he wanted to give in to those feelings, explore where they might lead, the timing was wrong. He had to find a way to separate his attraction for Faith from the task at hand because if he didn't, they both might not make it through this ordeal alive.

NINE

Faith drove through the early-morning streets of Hope Island with a patrol car in front of them and another behind.

When they were safely off the island, the lead car pulled over and flashed his lights. A moment later, the second did the same.

It was as if they'd become trapped in a bad dream that wouldn't end. "It's eerie, isn't it? Do you think people have already started to leave the island?"

"No doubt. Most of the fishing fleet will have secured their vessels by now. It's way too risky to fish in these conditions. The ocean can become volatile."

JT's phone rang and he answered it without speaking, listened for a second, and then said, "Good." Once he disconnected the call, he dropped the phone on the console next to him.

"Will's team finished canvassing the house. They didn't find anything else. The good news is we weren't followed off the island, so we should be safe."

She tried to see the positive in what JT said, yet she couldn't believe someone who had killed four people would give up so easily.

JT clasped his hand in hers. "Hey, for the first time we actually have something to go on. We'll get him."

She turned to him and nodded. "You should try to get some rest. I'll be okay for a while and it will give me something to do to take my mind off what's happening in my life right now."

JT leaned back in the seat and closed his eyes as the lights of Hope Island disappeared behind them and the coastline along the highway took their place.

If they were truly safe, then why did JT seem so worried? He was good at what he did. If he was concerned about their chances of surviving, then she was terrified at the possibility of what might lay ahead of them.

They had been driving for hours when his phone rang again. He pulled over on the side of the road and stopped the truck. It was a little past three in the morning. They'd stopped only once to eat the sandwiches Faith had prepared and to switch drivers. He'd managed to get a couple hours of uninterrupted sleep that had worked wonders to restore his strength. With the exception of the pain throbbing in his side and his injured arm, he almost felt like himself again.

JT glanced over at Faith. She'd fallen asleep. He couldn't help but notice how beautiful and peaceful she looked.

JT snapped Ollie's leash on and quietly got out. Ollie could use a bathroom break and JT didn't want to wake Faith.

"I have the Austin police report," Will announced without preamble.

"That's great…isn't it?" Something didn't sound right in Will's tone.

"I hope so. I told the detective what happened here and he expedited it."

JT had a bad feeling he wasn't going to like what his friend had to say. "What do you mean you hope?"

Will hesitated and then said, "I spoke in depth to the detective now handling the case."

"Now handling the case?" JT interrupted. "What happened to the original detectives?"

"One's retired and has since moved to Nome. The other is a sheriff in a small town north of Amarillo."

Man this wasn't what they needed. "That's not good. We could have used their insight."

"Yes. Detective Riley is going to try to reach out to them and see if he can get them to call me..."

Was Will stalling? JT's uneasiness kicked up another level.

"What aren't you telling me, Will? You found something in the report."

The other man sighed. "It's not what I found in the report. With everything happening, I've just begun reading it. I'm going to email you a copy of it along with Teddy and Derek."

"Okay. What else? Just say it."

"Detective Riley is very current on the case. He told me in the beginning, the detectives were definitely working under the assumption the murders were part of a home invasion gone wrong."

"So what changed their minds?"

The length of time it took Will to answer did little to reassure JT.

"Faith changed their minds. Especially when she reported the calls. Something about them didn't sit right with the detectives. Riley told me it all seemed a little contrived."

Contrived. The word stuck in JT's head. Faith had obviously been telling the truth because the same thing had happened here. So why hadn't the police believed her? "What do they mean by that?"

"They said something about the calls didn't seem genuine, so they did a little digging into her life. Turns out, Faith had started working for Carl as his business accountant about three months before the murders."

Surprise rendered JT speechless for a moment. How could this possibly be true? She'd never said a word to him about working for Carl Jennings. "So what does any of this have to do with the murders?"

"Maybe nothing. Maybe everything. After the homicides and once Faith was no longer the accountant for Carl Jennings's business, the person who took over for her found some…discrepancies in her record keeping."

"What kind of discrepancies?" JT asked with a sinking feeling in the pit of his stomach.

"Something along the lines of a half-million-dollar discrepancy."

He glanced back at the truck to make sure Faith was still sleeping. "Are you saying they believe Faith took the money?"

"I'm not saying that at all. In fact, no one can seem to pin down when the money went missing. I'm just saying it's an interesting fact."

Not the word JT would have used. "I don't think Faith took the money and I certainly don't think she's tied up in those murders. Think about what has happened since she left Austin. There's no way she had anything to do with this." JT knew he sounded defensive, but he couldn't help it. After everything she'd been through, he wasn't about to let them pin a murder charge on her.

"I'm not saying I think she's guilty. I'm just giving you the facts."

JT took a second to calm down. He reminded himself that Will was just doing his job. "I realize that. What about the cousin? Did the police check into him? With no other living relative, it stands to reason he'd be the one to inherit the bulk of the estate."

"You'd think, but according to Riley, the family attorney told them something else. Rachel would have been the next in line to inherit. With her dying at the same time as her father, the estate went into a trust. Apparently, Carl left everything to a list of charities he supported. There's a board of directors appointed to disburse the funds. And besides, the police ruled Ben out early on. He was at a party across town. He couldn't have committed the murders."

JT ran a hand across the back of his neck. "This case just keeps getting better and better."

"You've got that right. Riley is sending over the list of names of the board members, but according to him, the detectives who handled the case checked them out pretty thoroughly and didn't find anything unusual."

JT struggled to keep his thoughts in focus.

"Oh, by the way, I heard from Teddy."

JT realized he'd forgotten to tell his partners what had happened. "How'd they take the news of the attack?"

Will chuckled. "They were both mad as all get-out but once they learned you and Faith were safe, they were okay. Teddy told me he read Faith's medical records twice to be sure he didn't miss it, but there was no mention of the doctor prescribing her anything other than pain meds."

This confirmed JT's suspicions. "I'm not surprised. There is no way any reputable doctor would have prescribed a drug like this for someone with amnesia, which leads me to my next question. Where'd the meds come from if not from the doctor who treated her?"

"I don't know. I'm still trying to track down the doctor to find out what he remembers. It may take some finagling."

"Let's hope you locate him fast. The sooner we figure

this out the better. It's been a crazy couple of days and I don't see it ending anytime soon."

"That's for sure. Where are you two anyway?" Will asked.

"Not too far out of Whaler's Point. We'll be there soon."

"Good. The sooner you have her away from all this the better. My friend has assigned four of his best men to meet you over at Mark's place. They'll be stationed outside for as long as he can spare them."

JT said a silent prayer of thanks. "I owe you for that, Will." He hesitated. "Have you heard any damage reports from Hatton Island yet?"

Will blew out a sigh. "I'm afraid it's bad. The hurricane slammed into the island at a category 3. Most of the communications have been down for hours, but from the sketchy bits of information that have been coming out, it looks like half the island may be gone. Thankfully, everyone got off in time. I can't even imagine how difficult starting over from nothing will be. They're going to need all our prayers to rebuild." There was a long pause. "Stay safe, JT. Hopefully something will jump out in the report, and we'll have some answers for you soon."

"Let's hope."

JT ended the call and stared gloomily at the lonely stretch of road. It seemed the more they uncovered about the case the more confusing it became, and he had a feeling they hadn't even come close to scratching the surface of what happened that hot August night two years earlier.

Faith opened her eyes. Since it was still dark out, she had no idea how long she'd been sleeping in that awkward, scrunched-up position.

Last night had seemed like a dream or, more to the

point, a nightmare. Yet here she was running for her life. Proof positive *he'd* found her again.

"Good morning. How are you feeling?" JT glanced over at her. Even from the truck's interior lighting she could see that lack of sleep had left its imprint around his eyes.

"I'm fine." The kinks in her shoulder and neck told a different story. Ollie had positioned himself on the center console next to JT. When he realized Faith was awake, he hopped into her lap and licked her nose.

Faith reached over and touched JT's face. "How are you? You look tired."

He smiled wearily. "I'm fine. I think Ollie's glad you're awake. He's been stuck with only me for company. We made a pit stop a little while back. I'm sure the little guy could use another one."

She stroked the dog's ears. "Thanks for taking such good care of him. Where are we anyway?" The truck's clock said it was just past four in the morning.

"Almost to Whaler's Point. I took some back roads to make sure we weren't followed."

She peered back over her shoulder but the only thing she could see was pitch black. "And were we?"

JT was quick to reassure her. "No. I haven't seen another soul on this road for hours."

"Has there been any news about…last night?"

He didn't answer right away. Something *had* happened. She could see it in his eyes.

"We have the police report from Austin. Will spoke with one of the detectives who agreed to send the files over once he found out what happened here."

Fear slithered deep into her stomach like a familiar yet unwelcome guest. There was something in his tone. "And?"

He grabbed her hand and squeezed it. "And we don't

know anything yet. Will is stretched pretty thin with the murder investigation and the hurricane so he's only given the report a cursory review. I'll get Teddy and Derek to read through it as well. I'm hoping they'll find something."

He hadn't told her everything. Had he found out something about her involvement and didn't know how to tell her? "Okay," she said slowly.

"We have your medical records as well. Just as we suspected, there never was a prescription ordered for Zyban."

Her gaze shot to his. None of it made any sense. "Then how did I end up with one...and who's been keeping it active all this time?"

"I don't know. Will is still trying to reach the doctor who treated you to see if he remembers anything unusual happening the night of the attack."

Faith glanced out the passenger window at the darkness. She couldn't dispel the uneasiness growing inside. Everything they'd uncovered so far hinted that what she believed happened that night was an illusion. Had her brain simply created its own version of events to protect her from the reality?

The sky had just begun to turn pink when JT pulled into the parking lot of a retro diner with bright neon lights. The sign flashed, "Mel's Place. Open seven days a week. Best burgers in town."

"It's been hours since we've eaten. Let's have breakfast, then we'll stop at the store to get some supplies. With Mark out of town, I doubt his fridge is well stocked."

He was trying hard to take her mind off things and she was so grateful.

She got out and stretched. Off in the distance, she could see the boat docks where a handful of fishing vessels were anchored.

JT followed her gaze. "In its day, this locale used to be

a huge port of call for merchant ships and whaling vessels, thus the name, Whaler's Point. When the ships disappeared, the town almost did as well. Still, there are several generations of fishermen who make their living at sea. Mark has tons of books on the history of the area." When he saw her curious expression, he added, "As you can see, I'm a bit of a history buff myself."

Faith noticed he wasn't wearing the sling anymore. "Where's your contraption?"

"I took it off. It made it impossible for me to drive comfortably. The arm's fine as long as I don't bump into anything." The shadows beneath his eyes told a different story. So did the grooves around his mouth.

"JT…"

He took her hand and tugged her closer. "To tell you the truth, it hurts like crazy, but I really am okay."

His smile sent her heart slamming against her chest. "We should probably change the bandage," she whispered, a little unsteady.

He stopped smiling when their eyes met. "Once we get to the house, we'll take a look at it," he said almost to himself and moved closer. His hand threaded through her hair, bringing her still closer. He was going to kiss her. She couldn't think of anything she wanted more.

Close by, a car horn blared, and they jumped guiltily apart.

Faith's hand flew to cover her pounding heart and JT laughed sheepishly. "I think maybe we'd better try to stay focused on what we're doing. We don't want to escape the person chasing you only to have a car hit us in a parking lot. Come on, I could use some coffee."

The bell above the diner's door jingled their arrival to the handful of patrons and staff. No one seemed particularly interested in them. The sign by the register said, "Seat

Yourself," so they did. JT took her arm and directed her to the back of the diner where no one else sat. He waited for her to slide into the booth and then he scooted in next to her, facing the door with the windows revealing the entire parking lot and the highway to their left. They could see anyone coming or going into the place.

"Can I get you two some coffee?" a pencil-thin waitress with a pile of orange hair on top of her head asked. She had to be sixty at least.

"Yes." JT glanced at Faith who nodded. "Make it two."

The waitress brought two cups overfilled and sloshing with coffee. "Cream? Sugar?"

"Both," JT said. "And could we see a menu?" The waitress dumped sugar packets and creamers on the table and left.

Faith emptied two sugars and a creamer in her coffee, before stirring it to perfection. When the waitress returned she brought a couple of menus and waited for them to decide, tapping her pencil against her pad somewhat impatiently.

"What's good here?" JT seemed to be the only one speaking for them but she just couldn't come up with any words. Her thoughts were spinning in a dozen different directions.

"We're famous for our Western omelets." She smacked her gum and grinned at them.

"Then make it two." He closed the menu and handed them both back to the woman, who left them alone.

Faith could feel JT watching her. "No one could have predicted the murders or my attack." JT's sleep-deprived, rough voice interrupted her tortured thoughts.

She took a sip of coffee. "*I* should have. With everything that's happened, I should have seen this outcome and never gotten you and Will involved."

He covered her hand with his. "You didn't ask for any of this to happen—it just did. Don't start taking the blame for what you couldn't have any way of controlling. He's used your guilt against you in the past, and it's time to put the blame where it belongs. On him. When we catch him, he'll answer for his crimes."

Their eyes met in a long, lingering look. Her heart melted. JT was such a good man. He'd been through so much in his own life yet he'd found a way to rise above his pain. Now he was going out on a limb to help her, and she owed him so much. He'd never once wavered in his belief in her innocence, even after the murders of those two officers. She so wanted to be the person he saw in her.

"You're just as much a victim as those two officers," he told her with conviction. "You didn't deserve any of this."

"I know that in my head, but in my heart, well, it's hard."

"I realize that it is, but if we have any hope of getting through this I need you to be angry. Fight. Don't give in to the guilt."

He was doing everything in his power to keep her safe. She needed to do her part and not give up.

"Here are your omelets. I hope you enjoy them. Let me know if I can get you anything else." The waitress set their food in front of them and hurried to help another customer.

JT pointed to her plate. "Better eat up. We need to maintain our energy level so that we can keep fighting." Faith's appetite had returned in full force, reminding her it had been hours since she'd last eaten. She polished off most of the omelet and toast. Two cups of coffee later, the caffeine caught up with her. She felt almost normal again.

"Ready?" JT took out his wallet and left money on the table. He rose to his feet and held out his hand to her.

"Yes."

"Good. We're almost there. God willing, this'll all be over soon."

He had no idea how much she hoped his words proved true.

JT pulled out of the parking lot and headed up the coastal highway. His phone rang and he answered it through the vehicle's hands-free speaker system.

It was Derek. "Where are you guys?"

"Almost to the house. We should be there in half an hour. What's going on there?" JT didn't miss the tension crackling in his colleague's tone.

"I've been keeping a close eye on the storm from here. The good news is, Tyler's been downgraded to a category 2 after all the damage it did on Hatton Island."

"That's something anyway." JT glanced over at Faith who was hanging on every word. "I think we need to go over the files as soon as possible before the weather deteriorates any further and disrupts cell service. Maybe we can do a conference call later this morning."

"I'm on my way back to the office now to pick up some things just in case the roads become impassable. I'll meet Teddy over at my place and we'll give you a call in a little while. I know you both have to be dead on your feet, so try to get some sleep. Be careful, JT. This person is unstable and things have started to escalate beyond what any of us could have predicted. Who knows how it's going to end."

Those ominous words stuck in JT's head.

Once he disconnected the call, Faith asked, "Do you think everyone will get off the island in time?"

"I'm pretty sure they will. We have an excellent team of first responders who help coordinate the evacuation and they anticipate just about every possible problem." Faith accepted his answer and went back to watching the handful of fishing boats on the horizon.

The sun had inched up further in the sky by the time he turned onto the winding road leading to childhood friend Mark Steven's place. The house itself sat perched high on a rocky cliff, allowing spectacular views of the ocean while offering much-needed protection against most hurricanes.

The first unmarked police car with two plainclothes officers inside was parked a little ways down from the house, off the road and hidden slightly behind a clump of maple trees. JT waved as they passed. As he rounded the final bend in the road, the house spread out before him and he sighed in relief. For the first time since they'd left Hope Island, he felt safe.

JT pulled Will's truck into the garage at the side of the house and then turned to Faith. She had her eyes closed. She'd been fighting sleep for a while.

When the garage door closed behind them, she opened her eyes.

"Come on, let's get you inside," he said gently before he grabbed their bags, and she followed him into the house. The pain in his side had continued to throb.

Faith noticed it as well. "Let me take a look at your side. You've been favoring it for a while."

JT dropped their bags by the door. "I think that's a good idea. There are some extra bandages in my bag."

She took out the bandages while JT unbuttoned his shirt and tried to ease it off. Every little move hurt like crazy. Faith set the supplies on the table and helped him get the shirt off the rest of the way.

Dried blood stained the outside of the bandage. It stuck to his side and he grimaced when she pulled it free.

She glanced up at him, worried. "Did I hurt you?"

"No, I'm fine. Just keep going," he said through gritted teeth.

Once the bandage was off, the wound was red and ugly, but at least it had stopped bleeding.

"I need to clean it before we put the new bandage on." She took the medicine the EMT had given them and gently dabbed it on the wound. JT winced. The stuff burned.

"I'm sorry, I know it hurts. I'm almost done."

He clenched his jaw. "Just finish what you're doing."

She taped the bandage in place and helped him put his shirt back on. "Thanks. It feels better."

Her hands rested on the button she'd fastened. "You're welcome." She was so close. If he leaned in just a bit he could kiss her.

JT cleared his throat and tried to do the same with his straying thoughts. He desperately needed to keep a clear head, but whenever he was with her, his thoughts scattered to the wind. The scriptures said there was a time for everything. Someday, with God's help, maybe there would be a time for them.

"I'm going to bring in the groceries and make some coffee. Want some?"

"No, thanks," she murmured. "I'm bushed. I think I'll just go to bed."

"I understand. Do you mind waiting here for a second? Let me scope the place out. Make sure everything's on the up-and-up."

She stifled a yawn as he went around double-checking the doors and windows, verifying that the house was secure. Outside the window facing the ocean, the second unmarked car had parked behind Mark's storage building.

"Everything's good," he told her once he went back to the living room. "Thanks to Will, we have plenty of police protection and even if the storm hits Whaler's Point, we're safe here."

She stood on her tiptoes and kissed his cheek. "Thank you. I don't know how I can ever repay you for what you're doing. What price can you put on getting your life back?"

His hands circled her arms, holding her in place. Their eyes met. She was thanking him, but she'd done just as much for him. She'd made him realize he wasn't dead, even though he'd simply been going through the motions of living since losing Emily. He didn't want to just try to get through each day anymore.

He leaned close and rested his head against hers. "You don't owe me, Faith. If anything, you've made me realize how precious life is. You've struggled to live every minute of the past two long years. It couldn't have been easy. You make me feel guilty that I've taken my life for granted. I don't want to anymore. I want to live every day without regrets."

TEN

No matter how hard JT tried, sleep proved to be elusive. Although his body screamed for rest, his mind wouldn't shut down. He stared at the ceiling and replayed everything that had happened in the last twenty-four hours.

By eight, he finally gave up, got out of bed, pulled out his laptop and set up shop in Mark's study. After going over the police report from the Jennings' murders for a while without coming across anything useful, JT went to the kitchen and made more coffee. It was just a little past nine in the morning and he needed to do something to clear his head. Making coffee filled that need. He'd poured his first cup when Faith walked in.

"Want some?" he asked.

"Mmm…yes."

He chuckled at her enraptured expression and pointed to the table. "Sit."

She took a sip from the mug of coffee he handed her. "Weren't you able to sleep?"

JT set down his cup. "Not really. I was tossing and turning mostly, so I finally gave up and started reviewing the police report. Teddy and Derek are going to call pretty soon to go over it with me."

"Did you find out anything?"

He wanted to ease her mind but he didn't have anything solid yet, other than what Will had discussed with the detective from Austin and he wasn't quite ready to share that with her just yet. "Not yet. But I promise once we have a better handle on things, you and I will go over everything."

She let out a sigh and accepted his answer with a nod.

"It's been a crazy few days and this is an amazing house. Mark is an excellent architect and he went all-out on the place. He also has a tremendous library with tons of books about the history of the area. Go have fun, explore the place, just don't leave the house without letting me know. Above all else, try not to be too concerned. Later today, I'd like to take you over to the local gun range and show you the proper way to shoot a weapon. Just to be safe," he added when worry crept back into her expression. "I want you to be able to protect yourself if needed."

He took his cup over to the sink. He'd just started rinsing it when his phone rang. "That'll be them now. I'll be in the study if you need anything." He waited for her to respond before leaving.

JT shut the door to the study and answered the call. "Hey, guys."

"Everything okay there? You sound a bit frazzled," Derek said without bothering with pleasantries.

JT wondered when he'd gotten so bad at hiding his feelings. "We're fine. I just didn't get much sleep. Is there any news from Hope Island yet?"

"I spoke to Will a little earlier. The winds have really picked up and the pressure's falling rapidly. At last count, he said they were registering ten-foot waves near the shoreline. At least the streets are empty. Everyone has gotten safely off the island. That's some good news anyway," Derek said.

"Yes it is. Well, I know you both are busy, so why don't

we get started. I'm hoping three sets of fresh eyes on this will help us find something the Austin police didn't…" The beep of call waiting interrupted him. Will's ID popped up on the screen. "Hang on a second. Will's calling. I'll be right back." JT clicked over. "I wasn't expecting to hear from you with everything you've got on your plate. How are things there?"

"I'm afraid the storm's just starting, but I wanted to call because I have some news. I located the doctor who treated Faith," Will said in a low voice. "He's practicing in Georgia now. He remembered the details of the case quite well. He was very clear. He never prescribed anything other than some mild pain meds. He has no idea how his name got on the prescription."

"Clearly, someone kept the prescription current."

"Obviously. I'm working on getting a list of hospital personnel who might have worked that night. It's a long shot, but right now, I'll take a long shot. Let's hope the fingerprints from the SUV will solve our problem and give us a name. I've had my people go over every name on the trustee list. Everyone checked out. I think it's a dead end."

Despite his disappointment, an idea occurred to JT. "Do you mind emailing me the list of names?"

"No. What do you have in mind?"

"I want to show the list to Faith. Maybe one of the names will be familiar to her."

"It's worth a try and we don't really have much more to go on. I'll send it right away. I've left a message for Ben Jennings, but we keep missing each other. I suspect it has a lot to do with the hurricane." He sighed. "Cell service is terrible right now. I was surprised I got through to you. Anyway, the minute I hear from him, I'll let you know. How's Faith holding up?"

"Okay for now, but I'm not sure how much more she can take."

"Watch over her—and yourself. You're still a long way from being a hundred percent recovered."

JT knew this only too well. Even doing the simplest of things constantly reminded him of his injuries.

"The minute the storm clears Hope Island, providing the causeway is passable, I'm going to the island to check for damage. I'll call you when I have news."

"Great. Thanks, Will."

When JT clicked back over, Teddy asked, "Anything new?" Teddy had a lot at stake as well. He and Brenda had lived on the island most of their lives.

"Not yet, but the hurricane's just getting started. I'm afraid it's going to be a long twenty-four hours for Will's team and they could use our prayers."

"That's for sure."

Switching gears, JT got down to business. "Let's get back to the police report. Anything jump out at the two of you?"

"Well, Derek and I were just saying, from everything we've seen so far, the cops weren't exactly sympathetic to what Faith went through," Teddy began. "It's almost as if they believed she had something to do with the murders. And from what I've read of the report, it's shoddy at best and it's left me with a whole lot more questions than answers."

JT remembered Will had told him about the innuendos he'd gotten from the police in Austin. "Like what? What do you mean specifically?"

"For starters, the part about the home invasions on the second page." Teddy waited for both men to get to the page he indicated. "According to the cops, at the time of the murders there had been a rash of home invasions targeting several wealthy neighborhoods around the city. The perps took jewelry. Electronics. Anything they could fence quickly for easy money. Then there's the matter of the location. The Jennings home wasn't located in town like the others. They lived out in the country, quite some distance from town, in fact."

"Faith mentioned a fire had been started to cover up the murders." JT remembered thinking that was odd.

"Yes. With the exception of the one set at Faith's house recently, none of the other incidents included fire. They certainly never murdered anyone before. All the previous houses targeted were empty at the time," Teddy told them.

"Well, according to what Faith told me, the Jennings weren't supposed to be home, but their plans changed at the last minute. Clearly, they surprised the intruders—assuming there was more than one—by returning early and they panicked. Things got out of hand."

"Maybe." Derek didn't sound convinced. "But both victims' bodies seem to indicate they'd been dead for at least an hour before the fire started, which was limited to the living room alone. They'd have had plenty of time to ransack the place and take whatever they wanted. And there were some very valuable items in plain sight, according to the detectives, and yet they didn't take anything."

JT had to agree with Teddy. The home invasion theory didn't make sense, especially with everything else that had taken place in Faith's life since then. "Did the investigating detectives have any other theories? Any suspects?"

"From what I can see, the only person they ever really liked for the murders was Faith," Teddy said reluctantly. "I know you don't want to hear this, JT, but we have to check out all aspects of the case. From what I could gather, something about her story didn't add up from the beginning. The fact she was the only one left alive sent up all sorts of red flags. But they didn't have enough evidence to move forward and they couldn't get her off her story."

JT shook his head. He couldn't believe what he was hearing. "She's not involved."

"For the record, I don't believe she is, either. I'm just telling you what I know. I'm going to do some more checking. I know Will is trying to reach the two detectives who worked the case originally, but he has his hands full. I'm going to call my friend from Austin and see if he can put me in touch with them."

"That's a good idea. Do whatever you have to do. Hey, Derek, can you dig deeper into what was going on in Faith's life back then? Since she can't tell us anything about her past, you'll have to rely on whatever information you can find."

"Sure thing, pal," Derek said. "I'll let you know as soon as I discover anything."

JT glanced at his watch and was surprised to find it was late afternoon. They'd been at it for most of the day. "I had no idea we'd been working so long. I really appreciate your help. I owe you both big-time."

JT pulled into the empty parking lot of the Whaler's Point gun range and he and Faith went inside. The place was all but empty. No doubt, most would-be customers were preparing for a possible hurricane strike.

The lone attendant, a man who appeared to be in his late fifties, barely spared them a look when he told them to use whichever lane they wanted.

JT handed her headphones and goggles for protection then he took out his Glock, released the safety and handed it to her.

"Stand up straight, feet apart, and remember, whatever you do, you may only get one shot, so aim for the heart.

Keep your arm steady and when you squeeze the trigger keep the movement smooth and easy. Don't jerk the gun. The only thing moving should be your trigger finger. Here, let me show you."

JT moved behind her, his arms circling her waist, and her heart beat a crazy rhythm against her chest. He was inches away. Close enough for her to feel the heat from his body. His hands covered hers on the weapon.

His breath tickled her cheek when he spoke. "Aim for the heart and try not to jerk the gun when you fire it." Was it just her imagination or was there a huskiness to his voice that hadn't been there before?

Faith turned slightly so that she could look into his eyes to be sure. She caught her breath as their eyes locked, their arms still suspended in midair. The gun in her hand was all but forgotten.

His blue eyes darkened with emotion. He moved slightly and then brushed his lips across hers. A deluge of emotions threatened to sweep her away and she closed her eyes.

The overhead intercom system squawked to life with an announcement that the range would be closing shortly in preparation for the upcoming storm.

Faith's eyes flew open and JT started to chuckle. Soon she couldn't help but join in. Before long, she was laughing so hard tears streamed down her face. She couldn't remember the last time she felt so carefree.

"Talk about bad timing," JT murmured. "I think maybe that was a sign from above…literally. Let's try this again."

This time he stepped back and let her do it on her own. Faith aimed the weapon while trying to remember all the things JT had just told her. She held her breath and pulled the Glock's trigger.

"Good. In fact, very good," JT said, close behind her. She slowly lowered the gun. She'd never fired a weapon before. The thought of having to use it to defend her life scared the daylights out of her.

JT punched the button and brought the target to them. She'd hit the target dead-on.

"Nice shot. If I didn't know better, I'd say you've done this before. Why don't you fire off a few more rounds and then we'll call it a day."

"I can't believe there's a gun range so close to Mark's house," Faith told him as they left the building.

"This one's been here forever. When Mark and I were kids, our dads used to take us here." JT tucked the Glock inside his jacket and hit the remote-entry button to unlock the truck. Once they were both seated inside, he made no move to leave the parking lot.

Faith could tell something was on his mind. "What is it?"

JT took something from his bag. "This is my spare weapon. I want you to keep it close to you at all times, even when we're in the house. Remember what I said. You may only get one shot. Make it count."

Those words drove home the seriousness of the situation. "Okay."

Satisfied by her answer, JT turned on the ignition. Before they could leave the parking lot, his phone chirped and he answered it. Faith heard only his half of the conversation, but it was enough to understand it wasn't good news.

"What about the hospital? Can you get permission to check their database? Good. Let me know the minute you have anything."

"What happened?" she asked after the call ended.

JT put the truck in gear and they left the parking lot, merging into the light evening traffic. "That was Will. The results from the fingerprints came in. We couldn't find a match in IAFIS, the Integrated Automated Fingerprint Identification System."

Frustrated, she turned in her seat so she could better see him. "So what does that mean exactly?"

"It means whoever attacked me doesn't have a criminal record. His fingerprints aren't in the system."

The small amount of happiness she'd felt earlier at spending time with JT evaporated. "In other words, we're back to square one."

She couldn't believe it.

"Not necessarily. Will is getting authorization to check other databases like the one for all government and state employees. I suggested he try to get access to the hospital where you were treated. Most institutions such as hospitals require their employees to be fingerprinted."

She hesitated for a moment then asked the question she'd wanted to ask all day. "What aren't you telling me?"

He didn't answer right away and his reluctance spoke volumes.

"Is it bad?"

"Faith—"

"Please, just tell me. Whatever it is, I want to know."

"It's not bad," he said at last. "It's just…confusing. We've gone over your medical records. There's no prescription listed anywhere. Will spoke to the doctor who treated you. He never authorized the Zyban."

Faith tried to make out his expression in the dark. "I don't understand. Then how…"

JT shrugged. "We don't know."

She continued to watch him. "There's something else, isn't there?"

He chose his words carefully. "Yes. Will spoke with the detective who's handling your case now. He said you used to work for Carl Jennings. Why didn't you mention that before?"

JT was voicing the same old reservations that the Austin detectives had when she'd first told them about the calls. They didn't matter. He did. She looked away. "Because I don't remember anything about working for Carl. Because I didn't *think* it was important. Because I didn't want you to look at me like you are right now."

JT pulled the car over on the shoulder of the road and turned to her. "You're wrong, Faith. I'm not doubting you, and I don't think you had anything to do with your friends' deaths. I just don't want there to be any secrets between us. I need to know everything."

She shook her head. "I remember every single detail of that horrific interview with the detectives. They asked me questions like why did I suppose the killers let me live? Did Carl and I fight over the missing money? They even went as far as to suggest perhaps the reason I couldn't remember anything about that night was because I might have been involved. They said that maybe I only pretended to be the Jennings' friend." She released a shuddering breath. "JT, I thought they were going to arrest me for the murders."

Deep in some secret place in her heart, she wondered if they'd been right all along. She didn't think she could live with the guilt if that were true.

JT clasped her hand, compassion shining in his eyes. "That must have been difficult. After everything you'd been through, witnessing the murder of two people you cared about and not being able to remember it or your own attack, to be accused of causing their deaths had to be devastating."

She was close to tears. "It was horrible. They wouldn't tell me any of the details about my attack. They led me to believe they were trying to build a case against me. I was terrified. I couldn't eat. Couldn't sleep. When I first went to them to report the calls, I thought, surely they'd believe me now, but they didn't." She shook her head in dismay.

"They pretty much accused me of making the calls up to appear innocent. After he broke into my apartment and left the photo, I told the police I had to leave. I figured if they were going to arrest me, they'd do it then, but nothing happened. A couple of days before I left Austin, someone from Carl's business called to tell me they'd found the missing money. It had all been a mistake. The police never bothered to let me know."

"So the money was located?" JT was clearly surprised.

"Yes. Not too long after the murders, I believe. I was told it showed up in another bank account. The person who called me said he thinks it was all just a clerical error."

JT ran a hand through his hair. "There have been so many false leads in this case. Just when we think we're getting somewhere, it blows up in our face." He watched the rearview mirror as the headlights of traffic continued to pass by them. "Since you stopped taking the Zyban, have you remembered anything new? Even if it seems insignificant, it could mean something."

She didn't know where to start. With the drugs finally out of her system, her head practically swam with confusing memories. At first, she just assumed her mind was playing tricks on her until the memories became clearer. More detailed. Even as crazy as they appeared, there was no way she could have come up with them on her own.

"Have there been more than just the ones about the roses and the locket?"

"Yes."

"Why didn't you tell me?"

"Because they don't make any sense," she said, frustrated. "Since I stopped taking the Zyban, I'm remembering lots of things, but none of them can be true."

"What do you mean?" When she didn't answer, he said, "Why don't you tell me what they are? Don't try to analyze them. Maybe we can sort them out together. What have you remembered besides the locket?"

She stared out the windshield as a light rain began to fall. "You remember I told you Carl was a real estate developer at the time of his death, but his family made a fortune in oil before he sold the business after his son was killed in an explosion on one of his rigs?" When JT nodded, she went on. "Well, the part about Carl's son dying that way was never mentioned in the news reports, because I checked right after I started remembering things."

JT thought about that for a second. "The police might have mentioned it to you or you could have looked up the family's history online."

"Maybe, but I don't think so. The police weren't very forthcoming about Carl and Rachel. And after what happened, I couldn't even bring myself to read the news reports."

"Did the cousin mention it?"

She shook her head. "No, I'm sure he didn't. Like I mentioned before, Ben and I talked only a handful of times on the phone. Mostly we'd try to make sense out of what happened, but I don't remember us talking about Carl's past and I haven't spoken to him since I left Austin."

JT shrugged. "It's something. I'm not sure what, but at least it appears your memory's returning. Perhaps it was something Rachel mentioned. Is there anything else?"

There was. Something far more disturbing. Fear crawled up her spine at the thought of it, and she clasped her hands together in her lap to keep them from shaking. "I think someone was harassing me even before the night of the murders. I don't remember much about it—I'm not even sure if it is real or just a figment of my imagination. Maybe I'm just so desperate for this to end my mind is making up things." Her voice had grown tight.

A fragmented memory of those terrifying moments after she came home alone and walked into her bedroom… and he was there. She didn't have time to take more than a step away before he grabbed her. She'd tried to scream, but his hand clamped over her mouth. His hot breath fanned against her face. She'd clawed at him. He'd laughed at her attempts to escape. His hand tightened around her throat, squeezing the life from her. She grew faint. She'd been certain he was going to kill her and then he spoke. She remembered what he'd told her. "You belong to me." He'd played that terrible song over and over again.

"Why do you think someone was harassing you?"

"Because I remember it." Her heart pounded in her ears, her breathing grew shallow. She struggled to control the panic.

"Okay. Take a deep breath and try to relax."

She did as he asked. After several cleansing breaths, her heart rate slowed.

"Good, now tell me exactly what you've remembered."

She thought about it for a second. "I'm almost certain I was at the Jennings' ranch. For some reason I was the only one home." She glanced over at him. He looked shocked. "I told you it didn't make sense."

"You're right, it doesn't. Do you remember why you were there? Did you stay there often?"

She shook her head. "I don't know. Maybe it had something to do with the man who threatened me. I just remember I came home from…somewhere. I'm not sure what I'd been doing, but I was exhausted. I just wanted to crawl into bed and sleep forever but he was there waiting for me."

"What happened next?"

She swallowed hard. "He kept me hostage for hours, ranting that I belonged to him. The song—'I'll Be Seeing You'—it was his favorite song. He kept playing it over and over. He tried to strangle me, JT. I thought he was going to kill me. Then, as if flipping a switch, he kissed me good-night and left like nothing happened." She'd waited until she was sure he was gone and then she'd left town and went… She couldn't remember where she'd gone. As hard as she tried, she couldn't remember anything more.

"Did you report the incident to the police?"

She closed her eyes. "I'm almost positive I did."

"Do you recall anything about him?" JT pressed on. "What did he look like?"

"He wasn't very tall—definitely not as tall as you—and he wasn't muscular or stocky. I'd say he was kind of slim."

"That fits with the description you gave Will in the beginning. The problem is, it doesn't resemble the man who attacked me."

She stopped for a second, trying to get a good image of him in her head. "I remember he had blond hair, touching his collar and…" She touched her collar absently. His eyes had been the most disturbing. Filled with rage, they'd revealed the truth. He was mentally unstable.

"What is it?" JT asked.

"He had really dark eyes, almost black."

"Do you have any idea who this person is?"

She had to know him, she just couldn't remember how. "I'm not sure, but we obviously had some type of relationship. Or at least he believed we did."

JT took out his phone. "I need to show you something. It's a list of members of the board of trustees handling the Jennings estate. Carl left everything to a group of charities. Will checked the members out and none of them have records. I'm hoping perhaps one of those names might be familiar to you."

She didn't hesitate. "Okay."

He handed her the phone. "Take your time."

She silently read each name on the list and then stopped. Her hand flew over her mouth. Number four. He was the one who had terrorized her.

"Do you recognize one of them?" JT prompted.

"Yes." She pointed to the fourth name on the list. "Phillip Masters."

"Is he the one who held you hostage? The one you reported to the police?"

"Yes." Her voice was little more than a whisper. She remembered how petrified she'd been, certain he would kill her.

JT took the phone from her. "I'm just going to text Will and let him know what you remembered." Faith watched as he typed a quick message, then set the phone down. He was smiling when he looked at her. "Let's hope we have something useful soon." JT reached over and stroked her cheek gently. She closed her eyes and leaned into his touch.

"This is almost over, Faith. You're almost free of him." He leaned his head against hers and she was happy just being close to him. She wished that they could stay like this forever, just the two of them.

It felt as if a weight had been lifted from her shoulders. She believed him. For the first time since the nightmare began, she could almost see the end in sight.

Letting go of her uncertainties seemed as natural as trusting in JT. For this moment alone, nothing else mattered but being close to him. The troubled world melted away and it was just the two of them. And she was merely one breath away from loving him.

JT pulled back onto the road and headed back toward Mark's house.

She shifted in her seat so she could see his face. "Thank you."

He tossed her a quizzical look. "For what?"

"For believing me. For not letting me give up. For being so sweet to me."

He grinned. "You're very welcome. But, for the record, you're the only person to call me *sweet* in quite some time, so thank *you*."

ELEVEN

"I have some good news." Will's excitement was the first thing JT noticed when he answered the call.

He'd been watching the storm updates coming out of Hope Island on the TV. It slammed into the island as a category 2 a little past four in the morning. As expected, the storm took the island's power out right away. Although the reports were sketchy, the damage appeared to be widespread. The upside was the Weather Bureau had since downgraded Tyler to a category 1.

JT glanced at his watch. Just past seven in the morning. He muted the TV.

"I'm with the first responders and we're on the island now. They've opened the causeway to emergency personnel only. The electricity is out and probably will be for a few more days. The power company has crews on the island already." JT wondered what the good news was.

"Anyway, as we arrived on the island, we drove past the houses on Harbor Road. With the exception of a couple of trees down and some debris scattered around the yard, most of them are intact. When you talk to Liz, let her know her place is still standing."

JT had completely forgotten about the safety of their

homes. "Absolutely. She'll be thrilled to hear she has some-place to go home to."

Will chuckled. "I'm just happy to be able to report some good news. We're actually just passing along the beach near your place as we speak, and do you want to know the weird part? It's like every couple of houses are gone. Almost as if the hurricane took two houses and skipped one. I'm at your house now. Part of the roof is missing so I'm sure there's some water damage inside, but it appears minimal. God is good."

JT closed his eyes and said a quick prayer of thanks. "Yes, He is. That's amazing."

"It is. The last I heard, the storm's weakening, but I think Whaler's Point may still get hit with a glancing blow."

"I just heard the same thing. We'll be fine, though. This house is a fortress. Hopefully, the same can be said for all the folks in Whaler's Point." After hearing such good news, JT hated to bring up the case, but he couldn't shake the feeling time was of the essence. "Did you find out anything more on Masters?"

"That's one of the reasons I'm calling." Will's tone grew flat. "I spoke with Detective Riley. Phillip Masters is sixty-five years old and he doesn't come close to fitting the description Faith gave you."

JT felt like someone had kicked him hard in the gut. "Are you sure? I don't get it. I was positive he'd be the one."

"Me, too. There is one curious thing about Masters. Guess what he does for a living?"

"What?" JT wasn't sure what to expect.

"He's a prominent heart surgeon in Austin."

Masters was a doctor. That couldn't be a fluke. "You're kidding me. I wonder why it wasn't mentioned on the list."

"Because it wasn't pertinent to what he'd be doing as

a trustee, but get this. Dr. Masters was a lifelong friend of Carl Jennings and he has an airtight alibi for the night of the murders. He was performing open-heart surgery."

"You can't be serious."

"Sorry, buddy, but I am."

"Still, it's an awfully big coincidence and I don't believe in coincidences." It seemed like every time they had an ounce of hope, something came along and snatched it away.

"Yep. I don't think there's any way he's the person who's been stalking Faith, but I asked Detective Riley to talk to the doctor and do some more checking into his relationship with Carl." Will hesitated. "I have a suggestion to run by you and I need you to hear me out because it might sound a little bit out there, but, frankly, I'm out of ideas."

JT didn't like the sound of it already. He shook off his disappointment with difficulty. "What do you have in mind?"

"I have a psychiatrist friend who's worked with us on several cases. He specializes in treating victims of violent crimes. Specifically those who suffer from memory loss. I would like to have him speak with Faith and do a consult. I'm hoping he can give us some insight into what we're dealing with regarding her mental state. It won't be easy. She'll have to go back over some difficult details again and in light of what she's remembering now who knows what else it might dredge up."

JT sighed heavily. "All right. When do you want to try this?"

"The sooner the better. In fact, I spoke to him earlier and he's giving a lecture a couple of hours away from you. I don't think we can afford to wait, JT. I'll get in touch with him again and have him stop by this morning."

"Okay, but if she doesn't want to talk to him, I won't force her to. She has been through too much as it is. If

Faith doesn't agree to it then there's nothing I can do." JT wondered how he could ask her to go back there after all she'd suffered at this man's hands.

"Understood. Oh, I almost forgot. I mentioned what you told me about the missing money being found. Detective Riley checked on it. He confirmed the money turned up in a different bank account. It appears to have been a clerical error." He paused. "I hate to be the bearer of more bad news, but my friend, the Whaler's Point chief of police, is pulling his officers off the watch this morning. He's worried about high winds and storm surge. He needs all available personnel."

"Great. This just keeps getting better," JT muttered.

"I know and I'm sorry. By the way, I'm still waiting to speak to the cousin. He called late last night when we were in the middle of preparing for the storm. We've missed each other since. When I get in touch with him, I'll conference you in."

Faith was at the kitchen table drinking her third cup of coffee when JT found her. She'd been watching the ocean grow increasingly turbulent off in the distance. It seemed to reflect the turmoil in her heart.

JT pointed toward the ocean. "The wind's picking up out there. The good news is Tyler has been downgraded to a category 1."

"It's still coming this way, isn't it?"

"Probably. We'll be safe enough here."

Their eyes met. So many unspoken emotions passed between them. She stood and went to pour more coffee, but he caught her hand and held it.

"How are you holding up?" The roughness in his voice made her heart beat faster.

"I'm okay."

He stepped closer. "Faith…"

She closed her eyes against the storm of emotion in his. "It's just hard," she admitted slowly.

He drew her into his arms and she leaned her head against his shoulder. "I know it is. I hate that you have to go through this, but it won't be long before this is all just a bad memory. And then…"

The unspoken words teased her with possibilities. Just for a moment, she let her imagination take her to a place she'd refused to go in the past. The future. "I can't wait." She raised her head and looked into his eyes. "JT, I can't wait for this to be over."

He cupped her face and kissed her gently. "Me, too," he said, breathing against her lips. "You have no idea how I'm looking forward to you being free to…"

Before he could finish, the doorbell rang, interrupting them, and she wondered what he'd left unsaid.

He didn't move. He just kept watching her. The warmth in his expression as he searched her face made her feel special. Cared for. Needed. All the things she'd missed in her life.

When the doorbell sounded again he let her go. "I need to get that."

"Why? Who is it?" she asked once she'd got a good look at him.

"A friend of Will's. I wasn't expecting him so soon. He's a doctor. Dr. Everett Blake."

Her eyes never left JT's. "Why is he here?"

"He's a psychiatrist, Faith. He's worked on several cases in the past with the Hope Island P.D."

He barely got the words out before she understood what he wanted. "I can't, JT." She shook her head as she backed away, feeling betrayed.

"I'm sorry. I know this is hard, but he wants to help you.

He's had some amazing results working with people who suffer from memory loss due to violent crimes."

She was literally shaking with fear. Was she truly ready to uncover those memories? What if she learned the Austin police had been right about her involvement in the crime? But if that were true then why was someone stalking her?

"All you have to do is tell the doctor the things you've remembered. Let him help you untangle their meaning."

"But what if—" She stopped and looked away.

"What are you afraid of?" When she didn't answer he said, "Just tell me. It doesn't matter what it is."

"How can you say that?"

"Because it's how I feel," he told her simply. "I care about you. I want you to know everything about your past—the good and the bad—so you can finally begin to heal."

"And what if I'm to blame somehow?"

"You weren't part of their murders, Faith," he assured her.

He didn't know that for sure…and if she had been embroiled in the murders, would he still feel the same way about her? "But what if I am? What if you find out I knew the person responsible for Carl and Rachel's deaths. Or worse. What if I'm mixed up somehow?"

His gaze never wavered. "I don't believe you're embroiled in this for one moment. Think about it. Why would someone be trying to silence you after all this time if you were the one responsible for their murders? You weren't involved, Faith. You're a good person."

It scared her how important those words were to her. She went into his arms and he held her tight. For the longest time it was just the two of them standing alone as the world outside raged.

"Ready?" he asked at last.

No, she wasn't. But Faith knew she had to do this for him, so she nodded her head and whispered, "Yes."

"I'll be right there with you. If there's anything you don't feel comfortable answering, then don't." He touched her face gently and smiled.

Dr. Everett Blake was a diminutive man with thick glasses perched below bushy gray brows. He looked as if he'd just stepped out of a research lab somewhere.

When he walked into the kitchen and spotted Faith, he smiled kindly and extended his hand. Some of Faith's reservations melted away.

"I'm Dr. Blake. It's nice to meet you. Thank you for letting me stop by today. I've had a chance to review your medical records, and I've been briefed on what's been happening in your life since the night of the attack. I want to assure you, Faith, I'm only here to help you."

She shook his hand. "Thank you."

JT looked at her. "If you're ready, I think we should begin. The weather's getting worse and I don't want to keep the doctor too long."

Faith nodded and followed him to the great room. She sat on the sofa and JT took the space next to her.

The doctor pulled up a chair next to Faith. "Try to relax." Dr. Blake's soothing tone broke the nervous silence. "Don't think about your answers. Tell me exactly what you've remembered so far."

"It started with the locket," she said, forcing the words out.

"Tell me about that," the doctor prompted.

"I remember getting it for my sixteenth birthday. My father gave it to me. It had a picture of my mother inside." She smiled at the memory. "He was so pleased with himself. It was the best birthday ever."

"What's your father's name?" The psychiatrist asked curiously.

She started to answer but changed her mind. "I don't remember."

Dr. Blake didn't press the matter. "Tell me what else you've recalled."

Faith swallowed back emotions. "I remembered Carl's son was killed on one of his oil rigs before the family left Midland. The news reports never mentioned it and I don't remember the police telling me about it. And I remember someone was stalking me before the murders."

"I see." The doctor stroked his chin thoughtfully. "Can you tell us about that?" JT sat quietly beside her while she answered the questions. She reached for his hand, finding courage in that simple touch. "He held me prisoner for hours, but it wasn't at my apartment, it was at the Jennings' ranch, I'm almost positive of that."

"And have there been any other memories?"

"It's okay," JT prompted when she hesitated.

She let out a shaky breath. "No, it isn't. When you asked me my father's name just now, I almost said Carl Jennings."

JT glanced at the psychiatrist who appeared as shocked by this as he was.

"What do you think that means?" she asked when she spotted JT's worried expression.

He did his best to reassure her. "I'm not sure. Just relax for a bit. Everything's going to be fine." JT untangled his hand from Faith's and got to his feet. "I'm just going to have a quick word alone with the doctor and then I'll be right back."

JT waited until he'd closed the study door before seeking an explanation. "What exactly do you think it means, Doctor? Why is she remembering Rachel Jennings's past?"

The doctor stared out the window and took his time answering. "I can't give you a definitive answer, but I can tell you I have never seen a case like this. Without talking in depth with Faith, I can only guess at what might be happening."

JT tried to keep from voicing his frustration. "Just give me your best guess. In case you haven't noticed, there's a hurricane bearing down on us. We need answers. Now."

"All right," the doctor sighed wearily. "I have two theories, neither of which is good. She could be shutting out all memories of her own past because of the brutality she suffered. She and Rachel Jennings were obviously close. She'd know the girl's past quite well. Her subconscious might be adopting Rachel's happier memories as her own, rather than dealing with what's happened to her."

JT wondered if the second theory was going to be any better. "And the other?"

"There have been some documented cases where a person who is responsible for hurting someone close to them has actually taken on the injured or deceased person's life. The mind's way of dealing with their crimes is to become the person who was injured."

"You think Faith is responsible for killing Rachel and Carl." As JT forced the words out, his thoughts went back to his earlier conversation with her. She was definitely worried about what they might uncover, yet there was no way he'd ever believe she had a hand in such a horrific crime.

The psychiatrist shook his head. "I'm not insinuating anything. I'm simply giving you my assessment. There have been several documented cases to substantiate this. I'm sorry. I realize neither of these two options is very encouraging but—"

"Doctor, I've seen the unmistakable fear in Faith. On

that first night when I found her dog, Ollie. When the truck was outside her house. The fire. She's not faking anything. She didn't have anything to do with the murders."

"I hope you're right," Dr. Blake answered. "Because if not, you have a very unstable woman on your hands."

JT didn't want to let his mind go there. "Okay, well, I appreciate your insight, Doctor. If Faith remembers anything else, I'll let you know."

"Good." The doctor headed for the door. "I should go. I'll see myself out. Please be careful. You don't know what you're dealing with." With a brief nod for JT, the doctor left.

Alone, JT felt more discouraged than ever before. He wasn't ready to tell Faith the doctor's assessments just yet. Instead, he typed a quick text message to Liz letting her know he was okay and that her house was fine. With everything that had happened, they hadn't spoken since he'd called her when they arrived at Mark's.

JT glanced out the window at the steady rainfall. The wind had begun to howl with renewed vigor. The Weather Channel predicted the outer edge of the storm would strike close to Whaler's Point—some twenty miles away—by midafternoon, which meant they were in for some high winds, heavy rain and possible power outages.

He checked his email and found a message from Will. There was no record of the attack Faith remembered reporting to the police prior to the murders.

Faith couldn't stop shaking. Why was she remembering someone else's memories? It was…insane. She'd never been so scared before.

She clamped her fisted hand against her forehead. How come she couldn't remember her own past? Had she lost her mind or was she simply trying to cover up her guilt?

JT came in and closed the door quietly. She had tears in her eyes and he knelt in front of her and took her hands in his. "Hey, we're just now starting to unravel what took place."

"I don't think I can handle it if I find out I had a part in their deaths," she said in a wobbly voice.

He sat down beside her and pulled her close. "You're no killer."

She leaned against his chest and listened to his steady heartbeat. "How can you know that for sure?"

He smiled against her hair. "Because I *am* sure."

"Then why am I remembering Rachel's past? It doesn't make sense. What did the doctor tell you?"

He hesitated a moment too long, further fueling her uncertainty. "What is it? Please, just tell me."

JT reluctantly filled her in on what the doctor had said.

"No." The word escaped in a whisper. She covered her face with her hands as sobs racked her body. The doctor just confirmed what she'd suspected for a while. She could be the real monster here.

Please, Lord, no.

JT held her tighter. "That's not what happened so don't go there. You are not responsible for their deaths."

She rubbed away the tears and faced him. She'd never felt so hopeless before. "You don't know that. JT, I think it's time we considered the possibility that what the doctor said might be the truth."

He didn't hesitate before shaking his head. "No. I'm not letting you blame yourself for this. You're a victim, Faith, not a killer, and I won't let you give up. I won't."

She wanted to believe him. Wanted to be strong. But everything they discovered about her past seemed to point to her culpability.

TWELVE

"Can you talk?" The undertone of excitement in Will's voice made JT sit up straighter.

He'd been in the study watching as the waves crashed against the shore off in the distance. It was just past midday. The outer edge of Hurricane Tyler was close. It was only a matter of time now. "What's up?"

"I have Ben Jennings on the phone. I'm conferencing him in."

JT breathed a silent "Thank You, God." Then said, "Go ahead."

It took only a matter of seconds before Will came back on the phone. "Ben, I've asked my colleague, JT Wyatt, who's assisting Faith, to join in the call. As I explained earlier, there have been several disturbing incidents recently that have led us to believe whoever tried to kill Faith two years ago is stalking her still and has increased his violence."

"I still can't believe it," Ben exclaimed, seemingly in shock. "I had no idea anything was happening to Faith. As I said earlier, I haven't spoken to her since she left Austin and she never mentioned the calls to me. How can I help?"

"We are hoping perhaps there's something you may have forgotten to mention to the police in the past. Maybe something you've remembered recently. Anything at all, even if it seems unimportant."

"Absolutely. I'm happy to help in any way I can. Off the cuff, I can't really think of anything new. As you can imagine, it was the worst night of my life. Even now, it's hard to believe they're gone. Everything changed that night."

Will was one of the best at interviewing witnesses. He knew all the right questions to ask to elicit the information he was seeking. "I'm sure it was difficult and I apologize for having to ask you to rehash the tragedy, but with Faith's lack of recollection concerning what happened, well, we're working at a disadvantage. Can you tell me how well you knew Faith before the night of August 14?" Will's question didn't surprise JT. It was standard to confirm a witness's report.

"Not very well, I'm afraid. Faith and I have never met in person, so I only know what Rachel told me about her. I don't believe they were friends very long…before." Ben cleared his throat.

"Did Rachel ever mention Faith having a problem with anyone prior to that night?" Will asked. He was trying to substantiate Faith's memory of the man who attacked her at the ranch prior to the murders.

"I'm not sure what you mean. Are you thinking my uncle and Rachel's death weren't part of a robbery, as the police believed? It always seemed kind of unbelievable to me," Ben confided.

"That's the theory we're working on." The chief didn't offer anything further.

A lengthy silence followed. It was hard to determine what Jennings's reaction to this news was. "I can't even comprehend what Faith must be going through, thinking she's responsible for their deaths," Ben said at last.

"You said Rachel and Faith hadn't been friends for long.

Do you know how they met?" Will asked. "They didn't really hang out in the same social circles."

"No, not really…" Ben stopped for a second as if he'd remembered something. "I believe it was when Carl's business accountant retired. He asked Rachel to hire a new one. Rachel told me Carl wanted her to take a more prominent role in the business. At the time, Rachel worked as Carl's office manager so she agreed to interview the potential accountants. Rachel said she saw Faith's ad online, interviewed her briefly and then hired her on the spot."

"Faith must have been extremely qualified for Rachel to hire her so quickly."

"I suppose. Rachel was quite pleased with her."

"Can you think of anything unusual about the days leading up to the night in question? Maybe something jumps out at you now as being odd that might not have seemed so at the time?" Will asked.

"Believe me, I've racked my brain trying to come up with something to help figure out who did this awful thing to my family…" Again, Ben hesitated and JT leaned forward. He knew something.

"Now that you mention it, there was something. I'm not sure how important it is, though."

"Why don't you let us be the judge? As I said, you never know what might be useful at this point."

"It was something Rachel said to me maybe six months before… We were at the ranch talking one evening, just the two of us, and she told me something scary had happened to her and Faith. I asked her what she meant and she said someone Faith used to date showed up at the restaurant where they were having lunch and made a big scene by demanding Faith go home with him. He said something about her belonging to him. It terrified Rachel."

JT wondered why Jennings hadn't mentioned this before now.

"You think it's important?" Ben asked.

"It could be," Will told him. "We'll check into it."

"I'll be honest with you, at the time, I forgot about it. When the police were convinced it was a home invasion, well, I guess I just didn't think it mattered."

JT grabbed a piece of paper and jotted down some notes. They would need to find out who Faith was seeing back then. Maybe with her memory loss, her brain had simply mixed up the name of the real stalker with Carl's friend, Phillip Masters. The only question was how to uncover this information. By her own admission, she didn't have many friends. They'd need to find some way of identifying the man, but at this point, it seemed like an impossible task.

"What about your uncle or Rachel? Were they having any problems in their personal lives? Did your uncle ever mention having any specific problems with his friend Phillip Masters?" Will asked, continuing with the questioning.

"Phillip? No...not at all. They'd been close friends for years. Why do you ask about Phillip?"

"His name came up in our investigation. I needed to rule him out." Will kept his answer as noncommittal as possible.

After another pause, Ben said, "As far as I know, everything was going great for both Carl and Rachel. Carl loved his work and Rachel was settling in to take over for him one day."

"I see. Well, I appreciate your honesty, Ben. I know this has been difficult for you. Thank you for talking to us."

"It's no problem. If you have any more questions, let me know. There's not a day that goes by I don't miss them both so much. I'd like to see the person responsible for their deaths pay for his crimes."

JT waited until Will disconnected Ben from the call. "This certainly corroborates Faith's memory of being held hostage at the Jennings ranch. I'm just wondering if perhaps with the memory loss she's confused the name. What I don't understand is why there's no record of anything being reported. She was very certain about reporting the attack to the police."

"I don't know. Clearly, Phillip Masters isn't our guy. You need to talk to her again, JT. Tell her what Ben told us. See if you can jog any memories free. She has the missing piece to solve this locked away in her memory and we desperately need it."

"I'll see what I can do." JT wasn't sure how much more Faith could stand. She was barely hanging on as it was.

"It's really starting to come down out there."

Startled, Faith turned to find JT leaning against the door frame. She wasn't sure how long she had been sitting in the great room staring out as the rain battered the wall of windows facing out to the ocean below.

"I'm sorry. I didn't mean to startle you," he added when her hand flew to her heart.

Something in his expression made her uneasy. "Do you think we'll be safe here?"

He shoved away from the door. "Yes. The house is high enough on the cliff. We don't have to worry about flooding and Mark reinforced the structure to withstand a category 5 hurricane. The windows as well. We're safe."

Once her heart slowed to normal again, she asked him, "Have you ever been in a hurricane before?"

"Oh, yes. Several in fact. When I was around fourteen, a category 4 struck Hope Island. It took years to rebuild the island. A couple of others have come close enough for us to suffer some damage."

"And yet you still live there," she said in amazement.

He laughed and she couldn't help but join in. Being with him made her happy. That had to be a good thing. "Yes. Call me a glutton for punishment, but I love Hope Island."

She could certainly understand that. "I saw the patrol cars leaving. They're needed in town?"

The laughter left him. "Yes. Let's hope Whaler's Point doesn't take a direct hit." He sounded tense. She couldn't help but wonder what had brought so much edginess to his voice.

Below, the sea churned up foamy waves onto the shore. The local stations were predicting Tyler was due to strike soon. It seemed as if everything were coming to a head, including the weather.

JT settled into the seat next to her. Even with him beside her, she couldn't seem to relax.

His fingers entwined with hers. "We're getting closer. It's only a matter of time now."

She continued to watch the rain fall. "You have no idea how much I want to believe you."

"Then do. It's going to be all right. Soon, all of this will be just a bad dream and you can concentrate on living again." His thumb stroked her wrist gently. It was just the two of them. They could be any normal couple enjoying a quiet afternoon alone.

Being with him made her happy yet she couldn't help but wonder what would happen to them once this nightmare ended. Was she just a client to him? She had to believe from the way he looked at her, touched her, that he cared about her. But would any of that matter once they identified the killer? How would she feel if he disappeared from her life for good? Pain seared her heart. She didn't want to think about losing him. He'd become far too important to her. She loved him. She swallowed softly and glanced his way. He was watching her. Had he seen what she wasn't ready to reveal to him just yet?

He leaned closer and kissed her tenderly and she knew she couldn't be wrong. He did have feelings for her.

Slowly he let her go. "I have news. I just got off a call with Ben Jennings." He waited for her to take this in before adding, "Ben remembered something we believe might help confirm your memory of being held hostage."

An unbelievable sense of relief swept over her. "That's good, isn't it?"

"I think so. He mentioned something that happened several months before the murders. It might be significant. He said Rachel told him about an incident that took place at a restaurant where the two of you were having lunch. A man came up to your table and demanded you leave with him. Rachel said you told her the man was someone you dated in the past. The man said you belonged to him."

She closed her eyes and concentrated hard. She didn't remember the time JT had mentioned, but she could almost picture *him*. He was so angry. So different from the man she had first met at the hospital benefit. That man made her feel special. Cared for. Safe. It was his profession to take care of people…

She opened her eyes. "He's a doctor, JT."

He stared at her in disbelief. "Are you sure?"

"Yes, yes, I'm positive." She stopped as another memory nudged in. "I think I met him at a hospital benefit. That's something, isn't it? It's a start, right?"

He didn't share her enthusiasm. "Maybe. The thing is, I told Will about your remembering the name Phillip Masters and the description you gave me for him. He checked with the Austin detective handling your case and it turns out Phillip Masters is a doctor."

"Then I was right. He has to be the person." Yet something was wrong. She could see it in his eyes. "What is it?"

"Phillip Masters is sixty-five years old. A well-known heart surgeon in Austin, and he was performing surgery the night the Jennings were killed. It wasn't him."

She squeezed her eyes shut, feeling as if her whole world had just collapsed at her feet. "No, he *is* a doctor, JT. I'm positive. And his name is Phillip Masters. He works at one of the hospitals in Austin. He has dirty-blond hair. Dark eyes. I went to see him at the hospital to break it off, and he lashed out at me. It's him, JT. I'm sure of it." She looked at him hopefully. "Maybe there's another Phillip Masters out there."

She could see from his expression that it was a long shot. "Maybe. I'll do some digging and see what I can find out."

THIRTEEN

Faith rolled her shoulders to relax her cramped muscles. She'd been sitting at the kitchen table, her coffee untouched, trying to make sense of the memories. It seemed once the floodgates opened, all her locked-away memories were rushing back. The only problem was none of what she remembered added up to the precious few things she knew about *her* life. Were they truly her memories or was she losing her mind?

She remembered very clearly the ranch outside of Austin. Her bedroom. Her favorite horse, Cinnamon. Her father gave her the horse for her thirteenth birthday. The only problem was those were not her memories. They belonged to Rachel. Was it possible she'd taken on Rachel's memories as a way of dealing with her grief? Or worse?

Outside the wind's howl grew more threatening. Even the weather seemed aware of the impending showdown.

"Want some more coffee?" She hadn't realized JT was there until he spoke. He was so exhausted. She doubted he'd gotten more than a few hours' sleep in days.

"Yes." She tried not to show him how worried she was, but those disturbing memories were still fresh in her mind.

He didn't move. "What is it?" he asked, watching her carefully.

She shook her head. "I don't know what to believe any-more, JT. Nothing makes sense."

"You mean the memories. Have there been more?"

"Yes." She could hear all the uncertainties in her voice. "I keep remembering things about the ranch and the time I spent with Carl. The vacations we took together and yet they have nothing to do with my past. Those are Rachel's memories. Why am I remembering my dead friend's past?"

"I don't know," he said quietly. His response did nothing to settle her nerves. "But I do know we have some of the best people around searching for answers."

He stepped closer and pulled her to her feet. She caught her breath at the tenderness in his eyes. She reached up and touched his cheek. He was working so hard to help her get her life back.

He drew her near, his arms circling her waist. They watched each other for moment. "I'm not going to let anything happen to you again." JT cupped her face and kissed her softly. She kissed him back with all her heart and soul. She loved him, but how could she possibly hope to have a future when she couldn't remember her past?

Faith reluctantly pushed against his chest and he let her go. They faced each other across the tiniest of spaces, their emotions raw, and she couldn't hide her doubts.

"Give us a chance, Faith. Give me a chance. I care about you and I believe you have feelings for me as well. If you do, it doesn't matter what the past held or where the future takes us."

She'd give just about anything for that to be true. "I want to believe you."

"Then do." She had never seen him so impassioned. "I know I'm saying this all wrong, and my timing couldn't be worse, but what I'm trying to say is, you've made me believe in things I thought were over for me after Emily's death. You made me believe in second chances. And when this nightmare ends, I don't want to walk away from you and I don't think you want to, either."

She didn't. "You're right. I don't want that any more than you do, but I have to know what happened in my past before I can move on. Once and for all, no matter what the truth may be, I need to know what happened to Carl and Rachel. I need to know I wasn't responsible for their deaths."

JT stared out the window in Mark's study. His emotions were all over the place. He wasn't sure when his feelings for Faith had turned to love, but they had. He loved her and he was scared to death he might lose her to the past.

He shook his head. He needed a distraction. He couldn't afford to let those feelings cloud his judgment.

He'd give the perimeter one last check just to make sure everything was battened down before the hurricane hit.

It was just a little past one in the afternoon and already the outer bands of the storm had reached them. Rain pelted the windows and the wind howled with renewed anger.

He'd left Faith sleeping in the great room earlier to check his laptop for any updates. There hadn't been any, which was in itself unsettling.

He cracked the door and peeked in on Faith. She lay curled up on the sofa. He slipped inside. The room was cold, so he grabbed a nearby blanket and covered her with it. She moaned softly but didn't awaken. She was exhausted both physically and emotionally.

After checking the windows to make sure they were secured, he left her alone once more.

JT unlocked the front door and struggled to keep it from flying from his hands as a gust of wind whipped through the house.

Outside, something tipped over onto the porch. JT

stepped closer to examine it. A small, brown-paper-wrapped package had been propped against the door.

He bent over and picked it up. Out of the corner of his eye, JT saw the outline of something moving in the distance. A figure perhaps, but he couldn't tell for sure through the heavy fog. The hair on the back of his neck stood at attention. He didn't like it. Was it possible…

He went back inside and locked the door before opening the package.

As he removed the final pieces of paper, sheer horror at what he saw there threatened to buckle his knees. He'd been here. The killer had been here.

Faith couldn't shake the unsettling feeling that someone was watching her. She'd fallen asleep in the great room. The room was empty. Was it just a bad dream? She glanced around the room, but nothing seemed to be out of place. The clock next to the fireplace read just past one in the afternoon. It felt as if time had slowed to a crawl. Outside, the storm battered the house relentlessly and she didn't want to be alone any longer.

The minute she saw JT standing by the front door she knew something had happened. He held a small picture frame in his hand. When she got closer, she saw it was the one taken from her house.

"Oh, no…"

He turned when she spoke. Someone had put a red X over her face. *Rest in peace,* written in the same red pen above her head, and *I'll be seeing you,* at the bottom.

Her hand flew to her mouth.

No. Please, no.

He'd found her. After all their precautions to keep her safe, he'd found her again and it had nothing to do with her phone.

JT went to her and he drew her into the protective circle of his arms. "Hey, it's okay. I'd die before I'd let anything happen to you." She could hear the steady beat of his heart. In his arms, she felt safe.

"I'm okay," she said at last.

"Is it the same picture?" JT asked gently.

She swallowed hard. "Yes. Where'd you find it?"

JT held the frame carefully by the corner.

"By the door. I wanted to check the locks once more before the storm got worse. I stepped outside and it was propped against the front door."

The bloodred X drawn over her face sent the urgency of the matter off the charts.

"I thought I saw someone running off in the distance but I couldn't be sure. I don't know how he managed to get close enough to the house in this storm to put it next to the front door."

She recalled the feeling of someone watching her. "Do you think he came in the house?"

"I don't see how with the door locked. I'm going to call the local chief of police and let him know we need his help right away. JT dialed the number, listened for a second, then disconnected the call.

"What is it?" Faith asked apprehensively.

"The storm must have knocked the phone lines out in town. I'll see if I can reach Will. I want someone to know what's going on here. Until the storm passes, we're sitting ducks. The Whaler's Point police won't be able to help. We're on our own."

Six-foot waves pounded the rocky coastline below, washing up debris from miles away. The wind screamed with a renewed fury.

It was almost as if Hurricane Tyler were determined to

get in one last punch before it disappeared into the history books.

The fear churning inside Faith was just as unsettling.

It was as if the killer were conducting some macabre opera, directing their every move. Only he knew the ending.

"The storm's getting worse. Why don't you see if you can find some candles or maybe a flashlight in case the power goes off? I'm going to make sure everything's secured outside."

While she searched through the cabinets and drawers, it was almost impossible to concentrate on what she was doing.

She'd put so many lives in danger thinking this was the right thing to do, but they were really no closer to finding out what happened and more people stood a chance of losing their lives.

"I think the hurricane has made landfall," JT said as he struggled to close the door against the wind and rain. As if to accentuate the point, the lights flickered once. Even though it was barely three in the afternoon, outside it was almost as dark as night.

"How bad do you think it will get?" Faith's voice was less than steady. Her nerves frayed.

"I don't know. It could blow itself out with landfall, or it could get quite bad. This one's pretty unpredictable."

She still couldn't believe this was happening on top of everything else. "The coffee's fresh if you'd like some. I thought I'd make us something to eat since we skipped lunch."

"Thanks. I could use something to warm me up. The temperature is dropping like crazy. It's…eerie." He came over to where she was, his gaze lingering on hers. "Can I do anything to help you?"

She handed him a steaming cup of coffee and cleared her throat. "No, I've got it. You're exhausted. You should take a break."

JT grinned for the first time and her heart did a little flip. "I do want to check in with Derek and Teddy. Maybe something's turned up by now."

Faith placed the Glock that JT insisted she carry with her on the countertop next to her while she went about gathering ingredients to make a quick beef stew. She knew there was a real chance the storm would take out the power and the meal might be ruined, but she needed to keep her hands busy.

She'd experimented with lots of recipes since taking her cooking class, but her favorite by far was homemade beef stew. There was something almost therapeutic about doing the simple tasks like chopping vegetables for a one-pot meal.

With the stew simmering on the stove, Faith went to the walk-in pantry to get the ingredients to make homemade rolls. Her entire body was on edge, reacting to every little noise as the wind continued to howl like a siren outside.

She grabbed the flour, baking powder and baking soda and started back to the kitchen when the lights went out without warning. Instantly, the pantry was plunged into complete darkness and she dropped everything. No flicker. Just a frightening darkness that made it impossible to see her hand in front of her. She'd left the Glock on the counter, along with the flashlight and candles.

Faith groped her way to the kitchen. She'd just reached the stove when she heard a crashing noise at the back door. The once-locked door now stood wide open. A gust of wind and rain covered everything close by, including her.

Then he stepped inside. She spotted something in his hand. A knife. Instinctively, she knew it was *him*. She felt her way to the Glock, her heart pounding in her ears, keeping perfect time with her movements. *Just a couple more inches. Almost there.* She had to reach the gun.

Her fingers barely touched the weapon's barrel when he grabbed her from behind and the Glock flew from her hand. Before she could scream, a hand clamped hard over her mouth. Just like before.

No. Please, Lord, no.

She clawed at the hand covering her mouth, her heart thundering in her chest. His arm tightened around her, cutting off her air. He held the knife against her side. She could feel its cold blade through her shirt. If she wanted to live, she'd have to find a way to escape. She drew air into her lungs and kicked him in the shin with everything she had. He let out a yelp and loosened his hold. The knife slipped from his hand and slid across the floor.

Faith scrambled free and out of his reach. Her foot collided with something hard. The Glock. Before she could reach it, he caught some of her hair and she went sprawling on the floor. Desperately, she crawled on her hands and knees. She could hear his heavy breathing close by. He was gaining on her.

With her hands stretched in front of her, she found the Glock, flipped on her back and pointed the weapon in the direction she believed him to be.

She wasn't going to die on his terms. She'd fight to the bitter end because she wanted to live. She had a reason to live. She had JT.

With the knife forgotten, he dropped to his knees, grabbed her legs and yanked her toward him. The weapon went off and he screamed in pain, but didn't let her go. He jerked her against his body and knocked the air out of her. His hand pressed hard over her mouth once more.

She could feel his hot breath on her face. "Did you really think I'd let you go?"

She recognized his voice. *She recognized him.* This was the man of her nightmares. She even knew his name. Phillip Masters, Jr.

Faith fought with all her strength, but his grip tightened around her waist. He staggered to his feet and pulled her up with him. She could feel him smile against her cheek. Her terror pleased him.

"Hello, Rachel. You seem surprised to see me. Didn't you believe me when I told you you'd never leave me?" She pushed as hard as she could at the arm restraining her and he laughed. She frantically tried to make sense of what he'd said. *Rachel.* He called her Rachel.

She struggled to hold on to the faintest of memories. They'd been close at one time. She'd imagined herself in love until he revealed the monster within.

"There's no need to be afraid. I'm not the one who hurt you." He laughed and her darkest fears became reality. She'd seen that expression a thousand times in her dreams. "I only want to talk." She knew this wasn't the truth. In the past, he never liked talking. Phillip loved showing his power through violence. Faith fought to keep herself from losing control. She couldn't if she wanted to live.

He pulled her closer. "No…" she whimpered.

"Let her go." A shaft of light from a flashlight hit her eyes, blinding her and startling Phillip. He loosened his grip a little more and she broke free. She ran toward the light and straight into JT's arms.

"Get behind me," he whispered without taking his eyes off Phillip.

"Who do you think you are?" There was no mistaking the rage in Phillip's tone. He took a threatening step closer. "You think you can replace me with him, Rachel? You'll never replace me."

"Please, Phillip, you have to stop this. Please, just leave me alone."

Phillip's anger exploded around them. "I'll never let you go. You belong to me. This will never be over until you're mine, Rachel."

He lunged for JT. Before JT could dodge the attack, Phillip plowed into him with the full weight of his body, knocking JT backwards. The gun and flashlight flew from JT's hand and skidded on the floor. Faith raced for the gun first and then grabbed the flashlight as the two men scuffled around the room, knocking over a lamp in the process.

Phillip attempted to strangle JT, but JT latched on to his wrist and twisted it, breaking Phillip's hold.

"Stop or I'll shoot," Faith yelled, training the flashlight on Phillip's face.

Startled, both men turned to her. Phillip stopped in midstride. The look of disbelief on his face was almost comical when he spotted the weapon in Faith's hand.

JT moved past Phillip and took the gun and flashlight from her, his breathing labored. "See if you can find something to restrain him with until the police get here. I think I have some zip ties and rope in my bag in the office. Can you get them for me? Here, use the flashlight app on my phone." He handed it to her.

Faith nodded and grabbed the knife Phillip had dropped earlier, along with her lost Glock, and shoved them inside a kitchen drawer.

With another fearful glance Phillip's way, she went to the study and found the zip ties and rope.

JT took them from her and handed her the Glock and flashlight. "If he moves, shoot him again." He waited while she trained the weapon on Phillip's chest. "Get your hands behind your back. Now," JT barked when Phillip continued to glare at them.

JT grabbed Phillip by the arm and twisted it behind his back. Phillip grunted in pain and stumbled against the kitchen island. Before he could make a move, JT forced Phillip's legs apart and did a quick search for any further weapons. Then he snatched Phillip's free arm, pulled it behind him and tied both hands together with the zip ties.

It felt as if time had slipped into slow motion, yet things around her were happening at a rapid pace.

JT led the raging man into the great room while Faith held the flashlight and kept the gun trained on Phillip. JT forced Phillip into a chair and tied him to the chair with the rope.

With Phillip secured, JT took the Glock from her and tucked it into the waistband of his jeans. Then he pulled her close. "Are you hurt?" He touched her hair, her face, trying to reassure himself she was okay.

"No, I'm fine. He didn't hurt me."

JT held her tighter. "Thank goodness, I was so afraid when I heard the gunshot."

She'd been scared out of her mind as well. "I remembered what you told me about using the Glock. Right before I pulled the trigger, he hit my hand and the weapon flew out of my grip."

"I'm glad you had the gun with you. It probably saved your life. I need to get the power back on so I can take a look at his injury. From what I could tell, it doesn't look too serious. The breaker box is behind the house." JT handed the Glock back to her. "Watch him."

"You," JT said to Phillip, "keep your mouth closed."

Phillip did as JT suggested, but the pure evil in his glare made it next to impossible for Faith to stay in the same room with him. This was the man responsible for killing four people and for terrorizing her life for two years.

It took only a matter of minutes before the lights flickered on and JT returned. "The storm is affecting cell service. Mark has a satellite phone and I was able to reach the police chief and explained what happened. As soon as the storm clears, they'll be on their way." JT carried a first aid kit over to Phillip and cut the shirt free of his shoulder. "It's just a slight graze. You'll be fine," JT said as he finished bandaging the wound.

With everything that had happened, Faith had almost forgotten about the storm. She could hear it still raging outside. Windows rattled. If felt as if the house might implode around them as hard rain battered the windows. The wind screamed around the side of the house, thrashing trees against it.

JT came to her and took her hand. They moved out of earshot of Phillip and JT tucked her into the shelter of his arms. "We're safe."

Even Phillip stopped his silent fuming and stared fearfully out the windows as the deluge continued to grow.

"How long do you think before it passes?" Faith asked.

"We're only getting a glancing blow from Tyler so I'd say maybe half an hour. Perhaps longer."

Faith couldn't stop shaking. She remembered Phillip. She'd imagined this moment so many times in the past, never truly knowing how she would react and now she just couldn't stop shaking. He'd called her Rachel.

JT's arms tightened around her. "It's over, Faith. It's finally over."

If that was true, then why didn't it feel over?

Once the storm passed and cell service was finally restored, JT contacted Will to tell him what had happened.

"Thank goodness you're both okay. I've been trying to reach you for hours. As it turns out, Phillip Masters Jr. is a doctor, too. He's a surgeon like his father and, as I'm sure you've seen for yourself, he fits the description Faith gave us of the man who held her hostage."

JT found it hard to believe what had just transpired. "I still don't understand how he tracked us down, in a hurricane no less. Not to mention how did he get past all of Mark's security measures?"

"It might have something to do with the power outage."

JT had considered that possibility, but his gut told him it was something more. Mark had installed a backup generator a few years back. It hadn't kicked in, either. That bothered him the most. "Maybe. Still, it's strange. Anyway, it sounds like most of the storm has passed. I spoke with your friend the police chief. As soon as the roads are passable, he's sending help. They'll take Phillip to the station for the interview. I'd really like it if you were there."

"We're on our way now. I picked up Teddy and Derek as well. We should be at Whaler's Point in a couple of hours. We'll meet you over at the station."

JT hung up the phone with a sense of relief. Hopefully, within a few hours' time, they'd finally have some answers for Faith.

Once the police arrived and the EMT was satisfied Phillip's injuries weren't life-threatening, they took him out to the patrol car and read him his Miranda rights.

"I understand you'll be sitting in on the interview, Mr. Wyatt? Do you need a ride to the station?" the officer who took their statements asked.

"No. I have my vehicle. We'll be right behind you." JT closed the door and went to the great room where Faith waited for him.

Something niggled at his mind. Since Phillip Masters

Sr. was Carl's friend, it made sense Junior would be acquainted with the Jennings as well. Was that how Faith had come to know him? If so, why did he keep calling her Rachel?

Faith had suffered from a terrible shock, coming close to death once more at this lunatic's hands. Giving her statement had been difficult. He hated having to ask more questions, but he needed answers for his own peace of mind.

He closed the door, went over to the sofa and sat next to her. "Do you remember how you met Masters?"

She sat up straight and looked at him. "Yes, we dated."

"Then why does he keep calling you Rachel?"

She shook her head. "I don't know."

It didn't add up in JT's head. "But you recognize him?"

"Yes."

"And he clearly recognized you," he said almost to himself. What was he missing? "I'm going to sit in on the interrogation and see if we can find out more from Masters. I want you to come with me to the station. You'll be safe there." He wasn't sure why he added the last part.

He gently pulled her to her feet, drew her into his arms and held her close. He'd give just about anything if they could just stay here for a little while, but there were still so many things that needed to be settled. He kissed the top of her head and reluctantly let her go. "Come on, let's find Ollie. He can keep you company."

Even though the brunt of the storm had moved out to sea before it reached Whaler's Point, the wind had done some damage. The power was out up and down the coastline. Debris cluttered the roads, making the drive into town twice as long. A sense of uneasiness gnawed at JT throughout the harrowing trip. He had gotten a good look at Phillip Masters's eyes and he was almost certain he wasn't the man who had attacked him on Hope Island. In addition,

Masters was quite a bit shorter, not to mention thinner, than the man who had stabbed him. Yet even if he wasn't the same person, he'd clearly been tracking Faith. JT didn't believe the murders and Faith's stalking were unconnected.

JT parked the truck outside the Whaler's Point police station. He took Faith's hand and they went inside together. JT stopped in front of the police chief's office. "He won't mind if we use it for a little while. I'll be back as soon as I can."

She managed a tiny smile. She'd been unusually quiet on the ride over. He wondered if she were having the same misgivings he was. He so wanted this to be over for her, yet as he headed for the interrogation room, the doubts continued to crowd in around him.

Why had Phillip Masters confused Faith with Rachel? It made as much sense as Faith reliving Rachel's memories unless… Impossible. What he was thinking couldn't be possible. Rachel Jennings was dead. Her body identified.

JT opened the door to the interrogation room where Phillip Masters sat cuffed to the table, defiantly refusing to answer any questions. They'd need to find a way to make him talk to find out why he believed Faith was a dead woman.

"I've called my father. He'll have my attorney answer any of your questions," Masters proclaimed arrogantly to a clearly annoyed Will.

When Masters spotted JT, his face flushed bright red and he became livid. "She's mine. Rachel will always be mine. You have no right to her."

JT turned his full attention to Masters. Phillip Masters didn't call to mind a stalker, but there was definitely a monster lurking beneath his polished exterior. He'd seen it firsthand. The only question left unanswered was this:

Did he have an accomplice or was Faith's stalking just a huge coincidence and totally unrelated to the murders?

"That's the second time you've called Faith Davenport by Rachel Jennings's name. Rachel is dead." JT watched the man's expression closely.

Masters made a derisive sound then. Unable to stop himself, he answered, "You have no idea what you're talking about. I know Rachel. Everything about her. There is no mistake. The woman I saw tonight is Rachel Jennings."

Will carefully laid out photos of Rachel and Faith in front of Phillip. While there was a slight resemblance between the two women, anyone who knew them should be able to tell them apart easily enough. "Rachel Jennings is dead. Murdered along with her father," JT repeated. "What do you know about their deaths?"

For a moment, Masters let his guard down. The anger inside him warred with the madness. The man was definitely unstable.

"You don't know what you're talking about. My father has hired one of the best attorneys in Maine. He'll be here soon. Until then, I have nothing more to say to you."

JT ignored Phillip's outburst. "I have one more question. How did you know where to find us? You couldn't have tracked us by Faith's phone. We made sure of that."

Masters's arrogance returned. "We followed you, of course."

Will and JT looked at each other. *"We?"* Will latched on to the word. "Who else is involved in this?"

Masters quickly backtracked. "No one."

He was clearly lying. "Check his hands." JT couldn't believe in all the chaos of the night they had forgotten one crucial piece of evidence. The man who'd stabbed him would likely have cut marks on his hands.

Will had one of the officers force Phillip's hands open. There were no injuries.

"Maybe you were mistaken about the cuts," Will said. JT knew better.

Will motioned for JT and the others to follow him out into the hallway while Masters continued to spout angry, venomous words.

"He's not the man who attacked me. He's not the same height or build. His eyes aren't the same, either. This isn't our guy," JT said the minute the door closed.

"That doesn't make any sense, JT. He's obviously the one stalking Faith. Are you positive he cut his hands?"

Before JT could answer, Will's phone rang. "Chief Kelly here." Will listened for a second and then said, "What? Are you sure? All right, thanks." He disconnected the call and shook his head. "That was the fingerprint tech. Phillip Masters's prints do not match the ones we found on the hood."

The four men stared at each other in stunned silence.

"I'm telling you he's not the man who attacked me, and I'm guessing he's not the one who murdered your men or Carl and Rachel."

"Then why was he following her?" Will asked.

"I don't know. Why is he so insistent Faith is Rachel?"

"Yeah, that doesn't make sense. He has to know Rachel's dead—of course he knows," Teddy said. "Even in the delusional state he's in right now, he knows. It was all over the news for months. According to my friend, everyone within a hundred-mile radius of Austin knew about the murders." He furrowed his brow. "Do you think he's transferring his feelings for Rachel to Faith? If so, then I don't think we're going to get much out of him."

"Probably not," Will agreed. "I've asked Dr. Blake to stop by and speak to him before his lawyer arrives. Since he came to the house armed with a knife, we can hold him on attempted murder, and I will see if I can confirm he tampered with Faith's prescription. Unfortunately, once his attorney gets here, we won't be able to talk to him. Barrett Montgomery may be a piranha and the biggest sleaze-ball in Maine, but he's the best attorney money can buy."

"Something else occurred to me on the drive over." JT hesitated because he knew how crazy his theory would sound. "How did he find us? We made sure Faith's phone didn't have a tracking device on it and, with the exception of you, Teddy and Derek, no one knew where to find us."

"Maybe he tracked you through your phone. Maybe he was able to follow you somehow," Will said at last.

JT didn't believe any of those scenarios were true. "I don't think so. I'm telling you, something doesn't compute here. I think we've been investigating this from the wrong angle all along." The doubt in the three men's expression didn't surprise him.

"We've been over every aspect of Faith's life we could uncover," Will said as he watched through the two-way mirror as Phillip Masters jerked against his restraints.

"That's not what I'm talking about. We've been digging into Faith's past, thinking this was about her. Because of the calls, we just assumed everything was connected." JT motioned toward Phillip's disgruntled frame. "But we barely skimmed the surface of what was happening in Rachel's life. What if we're wrong? What if the murders were about Rachel, not Faith?" Before Will voiced his obvious concerns, JT added, "There's no doubt in my mind Phillip Masters was infatuated enough with Faith to come after her—in a hurricane no less. I just don't think he committed the murders."

"He's obviously delusional and delusional people do dangerous things," Will reminded him. "Then there are the statistics. Two out of three stalkers end up committing a violent crime against their victims eventually."

"I know all this. I just can't help but believe we're missing something."

The gravity of the situation was reflected in Will's tone. "What do you want to do? We don't have a whole lot of time here."

If JT's instincts were right, they were quickly reaching the critical stage. Because if Phillip hadn't committed the murders, then a killer was still out there, and he didn't want to leave Faith alone for a moment longer.

"I think we need to dig deeper into what was happening in Rachel's life before her death. Call me crazy, but I believe Rachel is the key to solving this thing, not Faith. This has nothing to do with Faith Davenport and everything to do with Rachel Jennings."

FOURTEEN

With Ollie sleeping contentedly in her lap, Faith listened to the silence of the empty office until she thought she might go out of her mind.

Phillip Masters. She knew his name. More importantly, she recognized *him*. The minute she saw his face, she remembered the terror he'd put her through.

No, not her. Rachel.

He'd called *her Rachel*. He hadn't even hesitated, or thought about it for a moment, he'd simply called her by that name. Which could only mean one thing: Phillip believed she was Rachel. And the really weird part? She'd remembered pieces of Rachel's life, but she didn't remember her own life at all.

She sat Ollie in the chair next to her and got to her feet. The dog whimpered, then went back to sleep.

Outside she could see the rain-slicked streets of Whaler's Point, littered with debris scattered everywhere. In the distance, traffic lights flashed. The storm outside had passed. The one inside her continued to rage.

She leaned her head against the chilled windowpane. Her father's smiling face appeared before her. No…Carl Jennings's face. He'd lovingly clasped the necklace around her neck. The picture inside the locket was so much like her. Evelyn Jennings was the spitting image of her daughter. Her daughter. Not Faith.

Her fingers reached up to stroke the imaginary locket and another memory far more sinister replaced the happier one.

He'd seemed like a dream come true. Phillip Masters was charming, handsome and already a successful surgeon by the time she'd met him.

She'd been flattered in the beginning by his attention, even when he seemed jealous of the time she spent away from him with her friends. Ben. Even the moments she spent with her father. Soon the real monster beneath the debonair exterior surfaced.

And the threats began.

Her father finally convinced her to file a restraining order against Phillip when he broke into their home and held her captive.

But Phillip's father had more influence around Austin than Carl did. With a single call to the police chief, he'd gotten all the charges dropped. Even though the restraining order was still in force, most of the police were afraid of the powerful Masters family and Phillip Sr.'s wrath in particular.

In the end, it had become little more than a joke and she'd left her home in order to escape him. After months of traveling, and never feeling safe no matter where she went, there was silence again. It was as if Phillip had lost interest in her. She'd gone back home. For a time, everything was normal. It had been about a year before the murders and a couple of months before she and Faith had met…

Faith shook her head. None of this made sense.

Then, out of the blue, he'd called asking her to dinner. She refused, but Phillip could be so charming and persuasive. He told her he only wanted to talk, to explain. She'd needed to believe it was over this time.

She'd been wrong.

From the moment she walked into the restaurant, she'd known meeting Phillip again would prove to be a horrible mistake. He'd stalked her many times after that.

Those memories returned just as terrifying as ever. But those were not her memories. How could she remember in such detail Rachel's life while her own remained a mystery?

Had she made up the whole thing in her head to cover up her part in her friend's death, as the doctor suggested? Maybe none of those things had actually happened. Maybe they just existed in her head.

"Faith? Are you okay?" JT pulled the door open. Her expression was the first thing he saw. It alarmed him. She was close to the breaking point.

"No, no, I'm not. I'm not okay at all. I think maybe I'm crazy. Maybe I've imagined this whole thing. Maybe there never was a stalking." The fear in her eyes was palpable.

He stepped inside and closed the door. "You're not crazy. Phillip Masters was stalking you. I promise, everything is going to be fine."

"How can you say that? I haven't been able to remember a single thing about my own life and now, suddenly, I'm remembering my best friend's past. That's insane, JT."

"I know it's hard to understand." JT poured a glass of water and held it out to her. "Drink this."

She held up her hands in frustration then took the glass from him. After she took a long, slow sip, she set the glass down on the table.

"You're not insane, Faith." His arms circled her waist

and brought her close. "I know you're frightened but it's almost over," he added with a sincerity he didn't feel.

She moved away and he let her go. She needed space. He understood that.

"Why would I recognize Phillip Masters?"

"It stands to reason you'd know him. After all, Rachel was your best friend. I'm sure you would have spent time together with Rachel and him."

She wanted to believe JT but something more was on her mind. "Then what about the locket? Why would I recall that specific memory—that particular time Rachel spent with her father? I didn't even know Rachel when she was sixteen and yet the memory is so real. And there's more." She glanced at him. "I remembered more about what happened when I was attacked at the ranch, but it didn't happen to me, it happened to Rachel. I remember my—Rachel's—father convincing her to take out a restraining order against Phillip."

This bit of news took JT by surprise. "If there had been a restraining order, why wasn't it included in the record of their murders?"

"Because the Masters name carried a lot of weight around Austin. The police were afraid of making an enemy of him," she said. "Do you think that Phillip might be responsible for Rachel's and Carl's murders after all?"

It didn't add up in his mind. "I don't know. I'll have Will check on it. Give me a moment and then let's go home. It's been a long day."

She continued to watch him without budging. "JT."

"Please, Faith, let's not argue."

"Okay," she said at last.

He left her to gather Ollie while he stepped out to the hall to call Derek. "Check on a restraining order against Phillip Masters Jr.," he said when Derek picked up.

"How'd you find out about it? We just located the original order. I'm here with Will and Teddy and we're still going over the details of the order with the chief of police right now. For some reason the cops didn't see fit to include any notes about it in the file of the murder case. Makes me wonder if Faith really did report the attack at the ranch and it got left out of the file as well."

"I'd say that's a possibility." JT went on to explain what Faith had told him about Phillip Sr. being a powerful man in Austin who had a lot of influence on the police. Afterwards, he took a deep, bolstering breath, hardly believing what he was about to say next.

"Derek...there's something else I need you to do." JT made sure Faith wasn't close enough to overhear the conversation. "There's a glass on the chief's desk with two sets of fingerprints on it. Mine and Faith's. If she was in foster care, chances are her fingerprints are on file somewhere. I need you to see if you can match the ones on the glass to Faith Davenport."

His friend didn't say a word for a long time. "You're thinking..."

"That it wasn't Rachel Jennings who died that night. It was Faith Davenport."

Derek let out a low whistle. "If that's true, then why did Ben Jennings identify the wrong woman? It doesn't make any sense."

"I don't know. Maybe the killer planted something on Faith's body to convince him it was his cousin. Faith mentioned a locket in one of her recollections. With the fire, the cousin might have relied on the necklace as proof the body found next to Carl's was Rachel."

"If what you say is true and if what the Austin police concluded was correct, why would Rachel want her father dead? By all accounts, they had a good relationship. He certainly appeared to adore her. I don't get it."

JT rubbed a weary hand across his face. "That makes two of us, pal," he said.

"Well, it's becoming more apparent a lot of things about this case are not close to what we originally suspected. I can't see Faith, or Rachel, being mixed up in the murders." Derek sighed wearily. "The Austin police did a lousy job of investigating all the angles of the case. They latched on to Faith as their primary suspect and ignored all other leads that might have helped them solve this case."

He saw Faith coming toward him and hastily added, "I have to go. Let me know the minute there's news."

"Watch your back, JT. I don't think we've seen the end of this yet."

Unfortunately, JT couldn't agree more.

They made the drive back to Mark's place in virtual silence. JT read all of Faith's worries in the impenetrable silence hovering between them.

He wanted to reassure her, but he couldn't because if what he suspected was true, the real killer was still out there.

He unlocked the door and Faith headed for the stairs without so much as a word.

"Faith, wait."

She didn't look at him as she rested her hand on the bottom banister. "I'm tired, JT. I just want to go to bed."

"Faith, look at me." She didn't. He couldn't let her walk away like this. He went to her and turned her to face him. "I know this is a setback."

She closed her eyes. "It's more than that. What's the point anymore? Phillip might be sick, but he's not a killer. He was in love with Rachel. He didn't kill her or Carl. Certainly not those two officers. He wasn't the one who attacked you." She took a breath. "We both know how this is going to end, JT, and it isn't good."

He reached for her hand and entwined his fingers with hers. "You've got to keep fighting. You can't stop now."

"I don't think I can. I'm all out of fight," she whispered wearily.

"You can. If not for yourself then do it for me." When she didn't answer, he realized he needed to give her a reason to keep fighting. "For us. Do it for us." He hesitated only a second then laid his heart at her feet. "Faith, I love you."

For a long time she couldn't speak. There were tears in her eyes when she looked at him. "You don't love me. You can't."

"I can. I do. I love you."

The hope in her eyes scared him. She desperately wanted to believe him. "But you don't even know me. *I* don't even know who I am. I could be responsible for..." She didn't finish but he knew what she was afraid of.

"You didn't kill them, Faith, and I do love you. Believe me, that's not a word I use lightly. You're only the second woman I've cared enough about to say it to. I love you." She stopped resisting and he pulled her into his arms and held her close. "That's why I need you not to give up. Keep fighting. You have to be strong, Faith. I need you to be strong."

He kissed her gently then let her go. "Try to get some sleep. There are some things I have to go over with my team, but I'll just be downstairs in the study if you need me for anything."

She touched his face tenderly. "I love you, too."

His breath caught in his throat. "When this is over, we have a lot to talk about."

"Yes, and I can't wait." She leaned over and kissed him one last time then left him alone.

He waited until she closed her bedroom door then he made coffee and went back to the study. She loved him, too. His heart felt as if it would burst from his chest. She loved him. He had something to look forward to. And something he didn't want to lose. The reality of what was at stake weighed heavily in his thoughts. He was still staring into space when Derek called him back. "Anything?"

"You were right. The fingerprints on the glass don't match Faith Davenport's. I'm still trying to see if Rachel's are on file anywhere, but I don't think there's any doubt she's Rachel."

JT put his head in his hands. "So Faith Davenport died and Rachel lived. Why kill Faith and pretend she was Rachel? Why go to such an extreme? What reason would someone have to keep Rachel alive for two years while pretending she was someone else?"

"Maybe the killer has a personal connection with her."

"Perhaps." JT couldn't make any sense of it. "Did you get anything more from Masters?"

"Nope. He wouldn't talk to Dr. Blake at all. The attorney arrived shortly afterwards with the old man on the phone, furious with us for violating his son's civil rights. He's being arraigned in the morning, but we're hoping the judge will see him as a flight risk."

"What about the cousin? Has he remembered anything more?"

"I don't know, he's still not answering. I don't like it. I'll keep trying, but in the meantime, I called the Austin police and they're sending a squad car over to his place to check on him. Let's hope the killer didn't get to him first."

FIFTEEN

JT wasn't sure how long he'd been sleeping when something awakened him. He'd fallen asleep in a chair in the study, his cell phone still clutched in his hand.

He sat up straight and listened. Nothing but silence. The house was dark. Then he heard it again. It sounded like footsteps. Impossible. The house was locked up tight. He'd made sure of it. The clock illuminated the time. Three-thirty in the morning.

Ollie came into the room and jumped onto his lap. Why wasn't the dog with Faith? He hadn't left her side all day. Ollie let out a low whimper. The poor little thing was shaking. Something had scared him.

"What is it, boy?" JT stroked the Pug's ears. The collar had worked its way up Ollie's neck. JT started to tighten it when he noticed something odd. There was an object stuck inside the dog's collar. It had a jagged edge and it had rubbed the dog's neck raw. JT took the collar off and examined it closely. What he found made his heart go ballistic. Someone had planted a tiny GPS tracking device inside the collar.

"Oh. My. Gosh." JT set the dog down and then dropped the collar to the floor and smashed the device.

He started to dial his phone when he heard it. Heavy footsteps heading up the stairs. Toward Faith's room.

JT grabbed his weapon and slowly moved to the door. He'd left it open in case Faith needed him during the night.

His eyes adjusted to the surrounding darkness but still he saw no one. Then upstairs, a floorboard creaked.

He carefully moved into the hall and close to the stairs. He could see the door to Faith's room. It stood open wide. He'd partially closed it earlier when he'd checked on her.

JT took the stairs two at a time. Before he reached her room, someone slammed the door shut and engaged the lock. And at just that second, JT's cell phone shrilled to life.

"Wake up, Rachel. You and I have unfinished business." At the familiar sound of his voice, she forced her eyes open. The room was dark, but she wasn't alone. He was there with her.

"Where are you?" It had been inevitable. She had been dreading this moment since that hot August night two years earlier.

"I'm here. I'm right here with you. For always."

"No." The word slipped out against her will. She didn't want to die. She'd lost so much. Fought too hard to live.

"No, Ben."

His laugh held traces of the insanity her father had become aware of shortly before Ben ended his life.

"So, you finally figured it out. That's too bad. You should have kept taking your meds, Rachel. I went to a lot of trouble to manipulate Masters into keeping that prescription active. I wanted to protect you from those memories and you fouled it all up." He stepped into a sliver of moonlight. This was not the Ben who'd been like a brother to her. This was her father's worst nightmare. She remembered their terrible argument. Her father pleading for her life. Faith's untimely arrival. Their deaths.

Someone yanked at her bedroom door. JT. *No. Please God, no.*

Ben read all her fears. "You remember what I did to your father and that meddling friend of yours. She was going to report me to the police if your father didn't. She had no idea who she was messing with. I fixed it so she took the blame, but she wouldn't let it go. She squealed to your father." Ben came closer. Terrified, she stumbled to the far side of the bed, but his fingers caught the edge of her gown.

JT continued to pound on the door.

"He's next, Rachel." He laughed as she fought wildly to free herself from his grasp.

Ben slid across the bed and pulled her up against him. The cold blade of his knife nicked her throat. Only a tiny whimper escaped before she forced herself to relax.

"That's better. Don't worry. You'll be dead before he can help you," he whispered against her ear.

"I'm sorry, love, but you have to die. You went to the police." Ben's grip tightened on her. "It wasn't supposed to be like this, but you left me no choice. That's when I decided you had to die, and I'd already set up Phillip as the perfect patsy. He was so easy to control. I just had to dangle you in front of him and he'd do whatever I wanted."

"Wha...what did you do?" she gasped, desperately stalling for time.

"I promised him he'd be with you and he jumped to fill the prescriptions. He even made those calls to you. He was already stalking you by that time, but when you left Austin after Carl and Faith died, he lost you. I told him where to find you. Thanks to Ollie's collar. I even told him what he should do to you each time." His eyes gleamed with sadistic delight. "The candlelit dinner. The photo. He thought he was wooing you. Only I knew those things would send you running for your life."

Ben laughed and it sounded maniacal. "I even made sure he wore the ski mask the night he broke into your house in Kansas. It was a nice touch, don't you think? I knew that even though you didn't remember him, you'd be able to recognize his height and build so that you could identify him one day." He smiled smugly. "He had no idea I was setting him up to take the fall for the murders. It would have all worked perfectly if you hadn't botched it up by stopping the meds."

Outside the door, it sounded as if JT put the full weight of his body against the door. It gave a little more and a tiny whimper escaped from deep inside her.

"You should have left things alone, Rachel. We could have been so happy if you had married me when I asked you. I loved you. We could have had it all. Your father's money. Our undying love."

Her eyes darted to the door once more.

"Are you listening to me?" The knife nicked at her throat again. She could feel a trickle of blood slip from its edge and land on her arm. Ben's hand holding the knife was unsteady. He was almost completely gone now.

"I loved you, you spoiled little brat. We could have been so happy but you refused to move away from Daddy. Even when he threatened to have me arrested for stealing the money that should have been mine all along. The money *he* took from my mother. I should have killed you when I had the chance that night, but I couldn't because I loved you and I believed we could still make it work." His voice trembled with rage. "It would have if only you'd kept taking your meds. In time, I knew I could convince you Phillip killed your father and Faith."

The door shook underneath JT's weight and finally gave way. In a splinter of wood and metal, it shattered off its hinges and into dozens of pieces.

JT raced into the room. The knife tightened against her throat. From somewhere close by she heard the sharp repeated rap of gunfire. Saw the flash from the barrel. *Don't let it be too late.* Then the knife sliced across her throat. The world around her swirled into a familiar darkness.

The past repeated itself.

"I'm sorry, Faith. I'm so sorry you had to die," Rachel whispered into the filmy darkness. Faith Davenport's life was cut short and Rachel's spared because of the affections of a madman.

She stopped fighting the pain. She'd been struggling to understand the past for so long and now she knew. She could stop fighting now.

The shrill of a siren blaring close by registered within her subconscious. Close by, someone spoke softly to her. Someone familiar. JT.

"Hold on, Faith." He still called her Faith. Did he still believe she was Faith?

"No." She tried to force the words out to explain.

"Open your eyes, Faith."

"No." Faith was dead and she wasn't who he thought her to be.

"I know it hurts, but the wound is only superficial. You're safe. It's over, Faith. It's really over."

"No." He didn't understand at all. It wasn't close to being over. It had only begun. She had only begun to remember who *she* really was.

Rachel opened her eyes. JT looked at her with so much love that she wanted to cry. It wasn't for her. He loved Faith. He didn't know who she was.

"Don't cry. I promise it will be okay."

"No, it won't. It will never be okay again. I'm not Faith." She spoke the truth aloud, yet his expression didn't change one little bit. It still radiated love.

"Faith…" Before he could finish what he wanted to say, the paramedics arrived to examine her.

"I'll be right here with you," JT assured her.

She glanced away…because she didn't want him to see her cry.

"It doesn't appear to be serious. We'll bandage it. When we get to the hospital, the E.R. doctor will want to examine you further to make sure," one of the paramedics told her.

"No." She needed to be alone. The memories of her past had become like a tidal wave. She needed time to sort them out.

"Faith, they need to make sure you're all right. Let these people help you."

"No. I don't want to go to the hospital." Close by, Rachel could hear the blare of another siren growing faint as it disappeared in the distance. It was taking someone else to the hospital. Ben.

"Is he…?" Even though he'd caused her so much heartache, she still couldn't hate him. He was sick. Her father had known this. Carl wouldn't want his nephew to suffer no matter what.

"He'll live. The shot was clean."

Will stopped next to JT and spoke in a low voice. "We're going to the hospital to wait for Ben Jennings to be released. Then we'll charge him with attempted murder to start with. With more charges certain to follow."

"Good." JT turned back to Rachel. "You're safe now. He's never going to hurt you again."

"I just want to…" She wasn't sure what she wanted anymore.

"Let's get you inside. You should rest." He brushed her hair away from her face, his fingers gentle against her skin. "Look at me." The tenderness in his voice forced her to do as he asked. "I know you're scared. A lot has happened, but it's over. It's finally over."

He waited a moment longer then lifted her into his arms and carried her back upstairs to her room.

"Rest now. You're exhausted. We can talk later. We have all the time in the world." When she still didn't answer, he settled for a kiss before leaving her alone.

SIXTEEN

JT couldn't believe no one had noticed it before. Ben Jennings had fooled everyone, including Rachel and Carl for a long time.

"Ben Jennings is one very disturbed individual." Will called the second there was a break in the interview. "Now the mask is off and it's easy to see he's capable of murder. He admitted everything. He was right there on Hope Island all along, keeping track of Rachel's every move. He was the one who shot at you. He planted the truck at Rachel's house, hoping to get her to come outside. At that point, he'd made up his mind he had to kill her because she'd talked to you. He confessed he'd been watching her since she moved to Hope Island. He knew everything about you and what you did for a living and he panicked. He attacked you outside your house as well. He was calculating enough to use Phillip Masters's stalking of Rachel to his benefit. Unbelievable." Will filled JT in on everything they'd uncovered so far.

As it turned out, Phillip had been struggling with schizophrenia for years. As long as he was on his meds he could function normally, but Ben had convinced him it was the medication that Rachel found repulsive, not him. It had been at Ben's suggestion that Phillip prescribed the drugs that helped to keep Rachel from remembering what really happened. Once JT came onboard, Ben got scared and realized he had to kill Rachel before she remembered what he did to her father and Faith. He planned to blame everything on Phillip. There was no evidence Phillip took part in any of the murders, but he had been stalking her for years and had continued to take part in her stalking along with Ben and at Ben's command. And Phillip did threaten Rachel with a knife so he would have to face attempted murder charges for what he did. The DA was hoping to gain his cooperation once he was back on his meds and more coherent. If he cooperated and testified against Ben, then he might get a lighter sentence.

"How's Faith—I mean Rachel—holding up? That's going to take some getting used to."

"Yeah I know. She's confused." JT couldn't imagine how hard it must be finding out you weren't who you thought you were for the past two years.

"Take care of her. She needs you, JT. We've briefed the Austin police. Once flights are able to land again, Detective Riley will come to Whaler's Point to interview Ben. We're holding him for the attempted murder of Rachel, but chances are the DA will approve his extradition back to Austin to face charges of first-degree murder in the deaths of Carl Jennings and Faith Davenport. Later on, the Hope Island DA will file murder charges against him for killing the two police officers."

JT shook his head. He couldn't believe everything that had happened in the last twenty-four hours.

"Oh, and get this, we found a pickup truck parked down the road from Mark's place registered to Ben Jennings. He had shoved the AK-47 under the front seat. We'll wait for the ballistics report, but I'm willing to bet it's a match for the one used on my officers as well as the attempt on you." Will took a breath. "We were able to get his phone records as well. The calls he made to me all came through a tower in Maine. He's been here for a while. Tracking Rachel since she moved here. For that matter, since she left Austin, thanks to that handy tracking device he planted in Ollie's collar. That was pretty ingenious for a madman. Anyway, if we can match the weapon with the shell casings, we've got Ben Jennings on first-degree murder charges for the deaths of my two officers. He will be going away for a long time."

JT pressed his lips into a grim line. "I still can't grasp what this lunatic was willing to do to keep Rachel quiet."

"Yeah, I've never seen anything like this one. When you and I talked to Ben on the phone, I had no idea he was our suspect. He was certainly good at hiding his dark side. He changed the story to Faith being the one Phillip had kidnapped that night. If you hadn't had the forethought to get her fingerprints, we still might not know the truth."

"It's amazing. He has all the makings of a serial killer. Who knows how far he might have gone to protect himself?"

"I'm just glad we caught him before he carried out his plan. I wish we could keep her out of it, considering what she's been through already, but we'll have to get Rachel's statement on the events of tonight and the Austin police will definitely want to talk to her now that she's remembered details from the Jennings and Davenport murders."

JT had expected as much. "I know. Can you give her some time first? She's been through a lot tonight, not least discovering she's not the person she thought she was for the past two years."

"I'll do my best. Take care of her."

Outside, clear skies made it impossible to believe anything bad had taken place there that day. Upstairs, he could hear Rachel moving around. He knew what was bothering her. It would be almost impossible to convince her his feelings hadn't changed, no matter what name she bore.

He found her fully dressed, staring out the window in her bedroom.

"Is he going to be all right?" She didn't look at him when she asked the question.

"Yes."

"He's sick. It wasn't his fault. My father knew something bad was going to happen. He tried to get Ben help, but by the time he reached out to him, it was too late."

JT came and stood close to her. She still hadn't looked at him. He could see her reflection in the window. She looked so lost.

"It's over, Rachel. You won't ever have to be afraid again." He tried to take her in his arms but she pulled away.

"It isn't. It isn't over, JT. It will never be over. Not fully."

"I know this is hard for you. It must be terrifying to find out what you thought you knew about yourself isn't the truth. But you're not alone. I'm here and I'm not going anywhere."

She shook her head. "You don't know what you're saying."

"I'm saying I love you. I'm saying whatever happened in your past is just that. The past."

"You don't love me." She forced herself to face him at last. "You fell in love with Faith McKenzie. Not me. I'm not Faith. Nothing about her is who I am. I'm not the woman you think you fell in love with, JT." She turned away.

"You're wrong," he said quietly. "You *are* the woman I fell in love with, Rachel Jennings." He turned her to face him once more and this time he didn't let her go.

"I fell in love with the woman who ran from me the first night we met. Who fought me every step of the way. The woman who taught me how to have faith again. And how to love again. The woman who changed my world for the better." He cradled her face in his hands and gazed tenderly into her eyes. "I fell in love with your strength, your courage, your overwhelming desire to survive. I fell in love with *you*. Not Faith McKenzie. Not Rachel Jennings. The woman you are right now. And I'm willing to do anything, whatever you need me to do, to prove it to you."

"JT." She desperately wanted to believe him. She needed to believe she wasn't her past or the lies she'd been told. She was simply herself.

"I won't let you go, Rachel. I won't let you run away from the future I know we can build together. I won't let you do that." The sincerity in his eyes melted away all her doubts. He drew her into his arms and there at last she stopped running.

"I don't want to anymore. I'm so tired of running. I want to stay with you."

"Then do. God brought us together, Rachel. That in itself is something special. We'll go back to Austin if you like. We can discover the person you were there, or we can let that woman stay in the past and begin our life together from this moment on. We can do whatever you want to do as long as we do it together. And as long as you love me."

Rachel pulled away a little so he could see the love she couldn't hold back any longer. "I do love you, JT. I love you, I love you, I love you—" His lips claimed hers, smothering her words. But it didn't matter. She planned to spend the rest of her life loving him, living the life she'd almost given up hope on having, and discovering who this new Rachel Jennings might be.

EPILOGUE

Six months later

"Are you okay?" JT asked once more as he watched his wife fight back tears. He stood close by her side at the family cemetery outside of Austin. Rachel had chosen to share the future with him and he'd never felt more blessed or more afraid. Their love was different from the love he'd shared with Emily, but it was just as strong and just as important to him. For the first time in a long time, he had someone in his life he couldn't bear to lose again.

Rachel struggled to answer him because the tears were falling freely from her eyes.

"She would be so grateful to you, Rachel. You did it. You helped to bring peace to her and your father. He would be so proud of you."

She reached for his hand and held it tight. She'd decided she couldn't change what happened in the past so why hold on to those painful memories.

JT had been by her side when most of the memories of her past returned.

"I still can't believe Ben would embezzle from my father. Dad treated him like a son and that's how he repaid him."

"In his own way, Ben was just as sick as Phillip Masters. He had it in his head Carl was responsible for his mother's death and that he'd taken Elizabeth Jennings's share of their inheritance once she died." JT shook his head. "He couldn't accept Elizabeth had gone through all the money on her own by the time she died. Ben didn't see it as stealing from Carl. He thought your father actually owed him the money."

Ben had confessed to embezzling funds from Carl's firm for months before Faith brought it to Carl's attention. Ben had manipulated the records to make it seem like Faith had taken the money, but Carl hadn't bought it. It had been the final straw as far as Carl was concerned. He'd confronted Ben. Faith showed up with the evidence. Carl was going to call the police. Ben panicked. After their deaths, and when he thought he'd gotten away with the murders, Ben put the money back into a different account to make it look like a clerical error.

"If I hadn't hired Faith, none of this would have happened. Faith would still be alive. She was my friend and I delivered her to her killer."

JT tugged her into his arms. "You couldn't have known what Ben was planning. He was desperate. He knew if he didn't do something he'd lose you as well as go to prison for a long time. He was just as obsessed with you as Phillip Masters and determined to have you and your father's wealth no matter what."

"But…"

"There are no ifs, ands or buts about it. He killed Faith and Carl…and there was absolutely nothing you could have done to stop him, Rachel. You can't take on his crimes."

He kissed her cheek. "It's over, sweetheart. Ben is paying for what he did. It's time to concentrate on the future."

There had been one final thing left to do. She and JT had returned to Austin to close the file on what had happened two years before. Rachel had decided to leave the business running the way it had been for the past two years and her father's estate would continue to go to charities. She wanted to return home to Hope Island, open her own bakery and be a wife and, one day, with God's blessing, a mother.

It hadn't really surprised him the way Liz had taken to Rachel. Within a short time, they'd become good friends. Liz was a natural-born mother hen, after all, and she'd played a tremendous part in Rachel's emotional healing.

Rachel had told JT that in some weird roundabout way, Ben had brought her to the island where she'd met JT and found out what it truly meant to love.

"Thank you," she whispered through her tears.

"For what?" he asked as they stood beside the headstone that now read "Faith Davenport."

"For giving me back my friend. For giving me back my father's love. But most of all for giving me back *me*. For loving me. For not letting me run away. Thanks to you, Faith can finally rest in peace. JT, you are a blessing and my Job moment. God promised He'd see me through this dark season if I trusted Him, and He did. Just like Job, He's blessed me with more than I deserve."

Although she didn't say the words, he knew. Rachel Jennings could finally start to live and trust again.

* * * * *

Dear Reader,

I hope you have enjoyed Faith McKenzie's incredible struggle to recover her past after it was taken from her in a brutal attack that almost ended her life and sent Faith running from a killer she couldn't remember.

In writing this story, I found myself overwhelmed by Faith's will to survive. I can't imagine what it would be like not to remember anything about the person you once were.

For Faith, moving to Hope Island seems like a desperate attempt to outrun the killer determined to finish what he started two years earlier, but God has a bright future planned for Faith. He brings security specialist JT Wyatt into her life to help her find the missing pieces of her past. With JT's help, Faith is able to bring the killer to justice and reclaim her life once more. And in the process, she finds the love of her life in JT.

No matter what darkness we face in our lives, we can rest assured God is right there with us through it all.

All the best,
Mary Alford

Questions for Discussion

1. For two years, Faith has been running from a danger she can't remember, changing her identity and moving countless times. Faced with the same obstacles Faith encountered in her life, what would you do? Have you ever been in a situation that seemed impossible to overcome? How did you deal with it?

2. Of all the places Faith could have moved, she finds herself living next door to a security specialist. When JT brings Faith's dog home to her, they are attracted to each other, even though both have suffered great tragedies in their lives. Do you think her move to Hope Island and the attraction they feel for each other is just a coincidence or part of God's plan for their lives?

3. Why do you think Faith finally agrees to accept JT's help?

4. What qualities of Faith's do you most admire?

5. After JT's wife was murdered, he didn't believe it would be possible for him to give his heart to another woman again. What do you think it is about Faith that makes JT want to let go of his guilt and learn to love again?

6. JT blames himself for Emily's death. Are there situations in your life that you blame yourself for or situations that you wish you had handled differently? How do you deal with these feelings?

7. What was the most unexpected part of the book for you? Why?

8. Both Faith and JT are struggling with past tragedies. How do you think those tragedies affect their relationship with each other?

9. Through all the moves Faith has made to elude her stalker, she prays that God will send someone to help her unravel her hidden past. She believes JT is God's answer. Has God ever answered your prayers in such a way?

10. JT has some very good friends and family to lend him emotional and spiritual support. Who in your life do you turn to for guidance and support? How do they help you?

11. Have you ever been caught up in a natural disaster, such as a hurricane? If so, how did you deal with it?

12. When Faith discovers the identity of the killer, amazingly she is able to forgive him. Have you ever been hurt by someone so badly and been able to forgive them? How did you find the strength?

13. When Faith realizes she isn't the person she thought she was, she believes JT won't still love her. Have you ever discovered someone wasn't who you thought they were? If so, what was your reaction? Did it change your feelings for them?

14. In spite of everything JT faced in his past, he turns out to be Faith's hero. He never stops believing in her

innocence and he is determined not to let her give up until the nightmare is over. Has there been anyone in your life you consider a true hero? Discuss.

COMING NEXT MONTH FROM
Love Inspired® Suspense

Available July 1, 2014

PROTECTIVE INSTINCTS
Mission: Rescue • by Shirlee McCoy
Someone is stalking widow Raina Lowery. But she has no idea
who or why. As the threats escalate for her and her foster son,
former marine Jackson Miller must do his best to protect Raina
from the past—and create a safe new future together.

SHAKE DOWN • by Jill Elizabeth Nelson
To Janice Swenson, the Martha's Vineyard cottage is an unwan
inheritance. Yet to Shane Gillum, it's the hiding spot for evidenc
to clear his father's name. But as he searches for answers, he fi
danger that puts their lives at risk.

FLOOD ZONE
Stormswept • by Dana Mentink
Dallas Black has to find a way to protect Mia Sandoval and her
young daughter from a killer on the loose and the perilous
floodwaters that threaten the town.

CRITICAL DIAGNOSIS • by Alison Stone
When army physician James O'Reilly returns to his hometown,
he finds himself protecting pretty researcher Lily McAllister fro
a ruthless stalker on her trail.

CAUGHT IN THE CROSSHAIRS • by Elisabeth Ree
When their simple mission goes horribly wrong, military sniper
Cara Hanson and Captain Dean McGovern go into hiding and
must work together to find the true culprit.

SMOKY MOUNTAIN INVESTIGATION
by Annslee Urban
Reporting on a serial killer turns terrifying when journalist
Kylie Harper becomes his new target. Now ex-boyfriend
Nick Bentley must risk his life and his heart to keep Kylie safe.

REQUEST YOUR FREE BOOKS!

2 FREE RIVETING INSPIRATIONAL NOVELS
PLUS 2 FREE MYSTERY GIFTS

Love Inspired®
SUSPENSE

YES! Please send me 2 FREE Love Inspired® Suspense novels and my 2 FREE mystery gifts (gifts are worth about $10). After receiving them, if I don't wish to receive any more books, I can return the shipping statement marked "cancel." If I don't cancel, I will receive 4 brand-new novels every month and be billed just $4.74 per book in the U.S. or $5.24 per book in Canada. That's a savings of at least 21% off the cover price. It's quite a bargain! Shipping and handling is just 50¢ per book in the U.S. and 75¢ per book in Canada.* I understand that accepting the 2 free books and gifts places me under no obligation to buy anything. I can always return a shipment and cancel at any time. Even if I never buy another book, the two free books and gifts are mine to keep forever.

123/323 IDN F5AC

Name	(PLEASE PRINT)

Address	Apt. #

City	State/Prov.	Zip/Postal Code

Signature (if under 18, a parent or guardian must sign)

Mail to the Harlequin® Reader Service:
IN U.S.A.: P.O. Box 1867, Buffalo, NY 14240-1867
IN CANADA: P.O. Box 609, Fort Erie, Ontario L2A 5X3

**Are you a current subscriber to Love Inspired Suspense books
and want to receive the larger-print edition?
Call 1-800-873-8635 or visit www.ReaderService.com.**

* Terms and prices subject to change without notice. Prices do not include applicable taxes. Sales tax applicable in N.Y. Canadian residents will be charged applicable taxes. Offer not valid in Quebec. This offer is limited to one order per household. Not valid for current subscribers to Love Inspired Suspense books. All orders subject to credit approval. Credit or debit balances in a customer's account(s) may be offset by any other outstanding balance owed by or to the customer. Please allow 4 to 6 weeks for delivery. Offer available while quantities last.

Your Privacy—The Harlequin® Reader Service is committed to protecting your privacy. Our Privacy Policy is available online at www.ReaderService.com or upon request from the Harlequin Reader Service.
We make a portion of our mailing list available to reputable third parties that offer products we believe may interest you. If you prefer that we not exchange your name with third parties, or if you wish to clarify or modify your communication preferences, please visit us at www.ReaderService.com/consumerchoice or write to us at Harlequin Reader Service Preference Service, P.O. Box 9062, Buffalo, NY 14269. Include your complete name and address.

LIS13R

For the first time in longer than Ryan Travers could recall, he was having trouble keeping his mind on his work. He couldn't have cared less about Jasper Gulch's missing time capsule; it was pretty Julie Shaw who occupied his thoughts.

"That's not good," he muttered as he stood on a metal rung of the narrow bucking chute. This rangy pinto mare wasn't called Widow-maker for nothing. He could not only picture Julie Shaw as if she were standing right there next to the chute gates, he could imagine her light, uplifting laughter.

Actually, he realized with a start, that *was* what he was hearing. He started to glance over his shoulder, intending to scan the nearby crowd and, hopefully, locate her.

"Clock's ticking, Travers," the chute boss grumbled. "You gonna ride that horse or just look at her?"

Rather than answer with words, Ryan stepped across the top of the chute, raised his free hand over his head and leaned way back. Then he nodded to the gateman.

The latch clicked.

The mare leaped.

Ryan didn't attempt to do anything but ride until he heard the horn blast announcing his success. Then he straightened as best he could and worked his fingers loose with his free hand while pickup men maneuvered close enough to help him dismount.

To Ryan's delight, Julie Shaw and a few others he recognized from before were watching. They had parked a flatbed farm truck near the fence beside the grandstand and were watching from secure perches in its bed.

Julie had both arms raised and was still cheering so wildly she almost knocked her hat off. "Woo-hoo! Good ride, cowboy!"

Ryan's "Thanks" was swallowed up in the overall din from the rodeo fans. Clearly, Julie wasn't the only spectator who had been favorably impressed.

He knew he should immediately report to the area behind the strip chutes and pick up his rigging. And he would. In a few minutes. As soon as he'd spoken to his newest fan.

Don't miss the romance between Julie and rodeo hero Ryan in HER MONTANA COWBOY by Valerie Hansen, available July 2014 from Love Inspired®.

Love Inspired® SUSPENSE

RIVETING INSPIRATIONAL ROMANCE

FLOOD ZONE

by

DANA MENTINK

Mia Sandoval's friend is murdered under mysterious circumstances—and the single mother is a suspect. Her only ally is a man she isn't sure she can trust. Search-and-rescue worker Dallas Black has a past as harrowing as Mia's own, and the police are suspicious of them both. With no choice but to work with secretive Dallas, Mia discovers he's as complicated as the murder they're forced to investigate to clear her name. Yet as a flood ravages their small Colorado town, a killer is determined that Mia, Dallas and their evidence get swept away to a watery grave.

Stormswept

Finding true love in the midst of nature's fury

*Available July 2014 wherever
Love Inspired books and ebooks are sold.*

Find us on Facebook at
www.Facebook.com/LoveInspiredBooks

LI44608